OTHER EYES WATCHING

For his latest invention, physicist Mason Brooks needs financial backing. To this end, he invites his wealthy sister Vera, and her fiancé Dr. Douglas Ashfield, to witness a demonstration. There is an explosion and the experiment goes horribly wrong, and Vera is not only blind, but has lost her eyes entirely. Then to restore her sight, Vera undergoes a dangerous surgical experiment which results in plunging all three of them into an astonishing web of mystery and intrigue . . .

JOHN RUSSELL FEARN

OTHER EYES WATCHING

Complete and Unabridged

LINFORD
Leicester

First published in Great Britain

First Linford Edition
published 2008

British Library CIP Data

Fearn, John Russell, *1908 – 1960*
   Other eyes watching.—Large print ed.—
Linford mystery library
   1. Blindness—Fiction 2. Accident victims—
Fiction 3. Surgery, Experimental—Fiction
   4. Detective and mystery stories
   5. Large type books
   I. Title
   823.9'12 [F]

   ISBN 978–1–84782–447–9

Published by
F. A. Thorpe (Publishing)
Anstey, Leicestershire

Set by Words & Graphics Ltd.
Anstey, Leicestershire
Printed and bound in Great Britain by
T. J. International Ltd., Padstow, Cornwall

This book is printed on acid-free paper

1

Matter into matter

There were only three people waiting in the reception room as the girl in the expensive powder-glass frock entered. She was a blonde, strikingly so, exquisitely made up, tall, and her figure streamlined into all the grace the beauticians of this advanced age could achieve. She carried herself regally, betrayed her high social order in every gesture. And with reason. Vera Brooks was worth many millions of dollars in her own right. It could buy anything she needed, except breed — and that Mother Nature had conferred upon her for nothing.

'Good morning, Miss Brooks,' the receptionist greeted her pleasantly, smiling. 'Dr. Ashfield won't be very long.'

'Important cases?' Vera asked, her bright gray eyes glancing towards the adamantly closed plastic door of the famous oculist's surgery.

'I'm afraid so.'

Vera nodded, reflected, then retired to one of the armchairs by the far wall. She had practically gone through four illustrated magazines before the last patient departed — then she got to her feet decisively, crossed to the surgery door and tapped upon it. Without giving time for a reply she slid gracefully inside and placed her exquisite form between a massive super-modern ophthalmoscope and a tall, dark-haired man with a sharply hooked nose.

'Good morning, Doctor!' she greeted, and Dr. Douglas Ashfield looked up in surprise to meet her impish smile.

'Why, Vera!' He clasped her slender hands earnestly. 'I am glad to see you again! Last I heard from you, you were jet-planing somewhere in the Pacific. I — '

'I wasn't intending to come back to New York so quickly,' she interrupted. 'I only got in an hour ago, and came straight here. It's Mace's fault, really. He sent for me; and you know Mace!

Anyway, I'm glad to be back, if only to see you again . . . ' The girl paused and glanced round thoughtfully at the optical instruments. 'Can you tear yourself away long enough to take me to lunch?'

'Can I!' Douglas Ashfield pulled off his white coat and hung it decisively on the walnut stand. Then as he buttoned up his cuff-studs his face became thoughtful. The girl had seen that look many a time before, when the firm lines of his still young face tightened and his keen dark eyes took on a meditative light

'I'll listen,' she offered, smiling. 'What is the great experiment this time?'

'Oh, just a dabble in mitonex lenses.' He shrugged. 'That is the new plastic Brassington found a couple of years ago. First class stuff for lenses — but I think it has other possibilities. It's the sclerotic coat which is worrying me now.'

'The only coats I know about are fur or glass,' the girl laughed. 'Incidentally, this frock is made of glass-powder. I bought it in Florida. How do you like it?'

She turned in a graceful pirouette. Douglas Ashfield looked at the frock absently, his mind on other matters.

'Nice,' he decided finally. 'Very nice . . .'

Then he jerked himself back to the everyday and hurried into his suit jacket. On the way out he told the receptionist that his surgery would be closed until evening — then with Vera hanging on to his arm they went out to her sleek dream of a car parked against the sidewalk.

'The Golden Comet,' Douglas told the chauffeur; then he settled beside the girl in the air-sprung cushions. 'I suppose,' he said, as the car sighed away from the kerb, that your brother is as peremptory as usual with his orders?'

'I'm afraid so,' Vera admitted, sighing. 'I don't think he realizes just how much he does rule my life. It may be because I'm eight years his junior — and that flatters his paternal instincts since mother and dad are both dead — or else it may be that he just loves power and the chance to order people around.'

Douglas smiled to himself, deciding that the latter was probably the case. He only liked Mason Brooks because he was Vera's brother, and for no other reason.

Brooks was the chief physicist in the organization known as the City Scientists. Impersonal, cold, he was about as friendly as the inhuman work he studied. And Vera, never very iron willed anyway, was more or less in his hands. She had money, yes, but so had he. In fact he was several million dollars ahead of her. Old Man Brooks had revealed himself as something of a throwback in believing man was still the dominant sex, and therefore entitled to the Lion's share of his huge fortune.

'Just why did Mason send for you?' Douglas asked when they were seated before the Golden Comet's most exclusive offering in lunches. 'Anything private?'

'I don't know whether it is or not. He's engaged on an experiment, which he says involves the subat — sub — ' Vera hesitated vaguely.

'Subatomic?' Douglas suggested.

'That's it! Something involving the subatomic waves of matter. He believes his idea will mean a great advance in science, and if that is so he is prepared to sink all his money into it — and he may

5

need some of mine too. So he sent for me. I am to witness this experiment. If it succeeds you'll see me writing a check before you can bat an eyelash.'

Douglas ate for a while in silence, rather wishing that he too had a wealthy sister on whom he could draw for money so freely when he needed it. Of course, the girl would soon be his wife, but he had the idea that a man in the real sense of the word does not progress on the strength of his wife's bankroll. He had money too, of course — he was a most successful ophthalmic surgeon and consultant — but it certainly did not amount to several million dollars.

'I suppose this experiment is exclusively for you and Mason to witness?' he asked presently.

'He didn't say,' the girl answered, eating daintily. 'You know how off-hand he is. But since it is at home in his private laboratory and not in the city physical research department I imagine it is private . . . Why?'

'I was just wondering if I could see it too — and decide if it is worth you putting your name to a check. I'm not much good at physics, I admit, but I'm not a bad businessman. I don't want to see my future wife depleted of her bankroll because of what may turn out to be a hare-brained scheme. I know what a dabbler Mason is: he's always at it! And so far he's never done anything particularly outstanding.'

'If you'd like to tell him that, you're welcome,' the girl said seriously. 'Personally I'd hesitate.'

Douglas considered for a moment or two, then, excusing himself, he went over to the visiphone booth across the room. In a moment he had switched through to the Brooks residence in Fifth Avenue and the manservant's face appeared on the viewing-plate.

'Mr. Brooks, sir?' he repeated, in response to Douglas' inquiry. 'Just a moment . . . '

After a while the physicist himself appeared, and Douglas decided he did not like the full-color image any more than he liked the original. Mason Brooks was lean-faced, with a droop to the corners of his thin-lipped mouth. He had the very long nose that often goes with the inquisitive mind, and very sharp gray eyes, the same color as Vera's, but with none of their carefree brightness. Intelligent beyond the average — this was clear from the remarkably high forehead and the dead black hair oiled down away from it.

'Hallo, Douglas,' he greeted briefly. 'You're lucky to catch me at home. I'm just having lunch . . . Something I can do for you?'

'Vera's back in town and we're having lunch at the Golden Comet,' Douglas explained. 'She's been telling me about your experiment.'

'Oh?' A vague surprise seemed to pass over Brooks' face. 'Well, it's right, of course,' he said. 'What about it?'

'Is it exclusive, or can I come too?'

'By all means, if you wish.' Brooks was none too cordial about it. 'I shouldn't have thought myself that a dabbler in mitonex lenses would have had much interest in deep physics. Still, if you want to improve your knowledge it's okay with me. I don't expect that dizzy sister of

8

mine to understand my work, but for certain legal reasons she has to be present.'

Douglas guessed that the legal reasons were connected with the possible need for touching her money, but he refrained from saying so.

'I'll come, then,' he promised. 'And thanks.'

'You're welcome,' Brooks said indifferently. 'In case Vera has forgotten it, the time is three o'clock. I'll be out until then.'

Douglas switched off and returned across the restaurant to rejoin the girl. She looked at him curiously.

'Been bearding the lion?' she questioned.

'Yes — and I'm coming with you. Three o'clock.'

'That will be a real prop for me to lean on,' she said, relieved. 'I hate these stuffy scientific experiments! Give me the open air, where I can tear through the sky in a stratoliner across the Atlantic. Anything like that!'

'I know . . . ' Douglas looked at her

with his serious dark eyes. 'You're a girl to whom life and movement mean everything: I've always realized that. I hope you're not going to find me an old sobersides when we're married. I shall have to stick to my work and my experiments, no matter what happens.'

'What men you and Mace are for experiments!' she exclaimed. 'But I promised I'd listen to you, didn't I? Tell me just what you are doing with this — this mitonex.'

'Well, you'll hardly credit this, but I think that with mitonex I can make something of everlasting service to humanity — create an artificial eye!'

The girl did not look impressed. She went on with her meal with youthful energy.

'That isn't so wonderful, Doug.' She shook her blonde head. 'An artificial eye has been going for ages.'

'Not a glass eye, dearest . . . An artificial eye that can see!'

She looked up at that, her pretty face startled.

'But that hasn't ever been done! In fact science says it just can't be done!'

'Douglas Ashfield says it can!' he replied. 'It's just the problem of the sclerotic coat which is bothering me a little. That's the white of the eye, you know, surrounding pupil and iris.'

'You think you can do this? Give sight to the blind?' the girl asked breathlessly; then as he nodded, her hand stole across the table and clasped his encouragingly. 'Now that is worth doing! It really is! So much more useful than Mace's crazy experiments which will be bound to blow him up one day!'

They both laughed — and thereafter, to the girl at least, the subject seemed to be forgotten. Douglas, knowing her somewhat wild spirit, knew that she had meant it when she approved his idea. But she had not the temperament or maturity for sustained enthusiasm over a subject she did not understand . . . By the time lunch was over experiments in artificial eyes and her brother's dabblings seemed to be furthest from her mind.

She insisted on an hour in the local news teletheatre and Douglas agreed, just to please her. When they emerged into the sunshine again it was 2.45 and the car was waiting for them. Punctual to the minute they were outside the door of the great Brook residence, isolated from the city in its own private grounds, at three o'clock.

The manservant let them in and did not look at all surprised at Vera's quick entrance. He was accustomed to her spasmodic comings and goings.

'My bags are in the car, Jefferson,' she said briefly, taking off the conical absurdity that passed for a hat. 'Where is my brother?'

Jefferson did not need to answer, for the tall figure of Mason Brooks appeared at that moment from the opposite end of the great hall. He stopped and gave the girl a dutiful kiss on the left cheek, then he seized Douglas' hand in a bony clutch.

'Decided to risk it, eh, Doug?' he asked dryly. 'Well, I can't guarantee that you'll be interested, but I can hope . . . You've had lunch, I think you said?'

'We're all ready for action,' Vera announced.

'Good! That saves any delay. Come

along to the lab . . . '

Brooks preceded them to a door leading off the hall and flung it open. To Vera the place was familiar, even though it was sacrosanct territory that she never entered except at her brother's request. To Douglas Ashfield, though not a scientist in the accepted sense, it was a fascinating vision. Mason Brooks' money had succeeded in making the place as fully equipped with every modern scientific device as the city physical laboratories themselves.

Brooks shut the door and came forward, stood with his hands in the pockets of his white overall. Then he nodded to a machine, which was obviously electrical in nature.

'I don't know whether either of you know anything about the constitution of matter,' he said presently, raising an inquiring eyebrow.

'I know a little,' Douglas answered as Vera shook her fair head bewilderedly. 'I know matter is composed of atoms and molecules — that nothing solid is really solid.'

'That, of course, is high school knowledge,' Brooks observed dryly. 'We shall need to go much deeper here. It is assumed by most leading scientists today that all kinds of matter can be penetrated if one has the right apparatus for doing it. I do not mean that a six-inch armor plate can be pierced by a high-velocity shell — but that, say, a six-foot cube of cast steel can be made to pass through another six-foot cube of cast steel without damage to either.'

'That sounds rather like a conjuring trick,' Vera remarked.

Brooks glanced at her coldly. 'I did not assemble all this apparatus and work myself nearly into brain fever in order to perform a conjuring trick, Sis, believe me! This conception is highly scientific, and I believe it is now perfect. If I can pass a solid through a solid without damage to either, the scientific and commercial possibilities will be endless. Man will be able to probe deep into the earth without any resistance; military equipment like the five-hundred-ton tank will be able to go right through the thickest defense wall

— The developments will be legion!'

'I can see that,' Douglas agreed thoughtfully. 'But how is it done?'

'Ah!' The physicist grinned cynically. 'Now we come to the deep part! Solids, as you remarked, Doug, are composed of atoms, and atoms, of course, are analogous to miniature solar systems. In other words, if you can picture them from a sideways angle they are flat. But, this flatness points in all directions — or, more concisely, it is not organized. Because of this no solid can fall through another: no two solids can be said to occupy the same space at the same time.'

'Clear so far,' Douglas affirmed, thinking — then he smiled as he saw Vera woefully holding her forehead.

'Now, atoms have poles,' Brooks went on deliberately. 'But these poles point in all directions. I have devised a system whereby magnetism can make them all point in one direction. By this means I can make the atoms all flat — parallel — so that they only block about fifteen percent of the space they occupied in their disordered forms. Under this influence one solid can go right through another, and the moment the transition is complete and the magnetism removed the atoms swing back into their former disordered state and solidity returns.'

There was silence for a moment, then Douglas nodded slowly.

'Yes — yes, I see what you mean. If you can do it, it will certainly be the biggest scientific achievement for years.'

A faint flush of pleasure crept into the physicist's pale cheeks. Praise for his work was the one thing he loved.

'It will take plenty of money to demonstrate it on a big scale,' he said. 'I have made so many bad experiments that the City Scientists haven't got a great deal of faith in me. That may mean floating a company of my own . . . Anyway, we'll see first how I go on. I know it will work because mathematics have proved it. Now, watch carefully.'

He switched on his peculiarly designed apparatus and displays began to glow. Bar magnets, too, took on a faint haze of energy. The dynamos crept up the scale and whined.

Fascinated, Vera and Douglas stood watching together as two automatic arms shifted two heavy cubes of cast steel along a specially made cradle. As they came into the area of the bar magnets they hazed visibly and the other side of the laboratory became faintly visible through them. Then, gradually, they began to approach each other. They touched. There was a faint surge of added power in the equipment — then the impossible began to happen!

Each block began to melt into the other, both of them narrowing their sizes as they came near to an identical fit. It was like a movie wherein a shadow image steps into itself.

'I think that proves it,' Brooks said, when one block was dead inside the other. 'Now we can — '

He broke off suddenly, his startled eyes on the power gauges.

'Hell!' he exploded. 'I forgot! The extra energy means an increased load on the magnets, and I don't think they'll stand it — ! I've got to tear these damned things apart before the fuses break — '

He swung, fiddling with the switches that controlled the block cradles. The two blocks began to come out of one another again, but they had only progressed about six inches before the dreaded thing happened. The overload blew the main fuses, with a decisive snap. Other things happened simultaneously . . . Two blocks of steel were suddenly both in the same space at the same time. The colossal energy produced by such a condition liberated itself in the form of a resistless expansion —

Douglas had just time to behold the whole apparatus apparently hurtling straight for him. He heard Vera scream as she reeled back with her hands clapped to her face. Somewhere behind a machine Mason Brooks was cowering — Then the laboratory attached to the Brooks mansion went sailing into mid-air and gave New York its most spectacular explosion for many a long day.

2

Synthetic Optics

For six weeks and more Douglas Ashfield had little real awareness of what was going on around him. People came and went like so many phantoms in the midst of chaotic dreams. It was only by degrees that he realized the truth — that he was in a nursing home, that three of his ribs, an arm, and a leg were broken that he had had concussion and complications. But the powers of modern surgery had saved him. He was commencing to mend.

Then at last the clouds of his illness began to evaporate. Weak but rational, he was permitted his first visitor — Mason Brooks. The scientist looked unusually harassed as he drew up a chair to the bedside.

'To say that I owe you an apology sounds idiotic,' he commented, as Douglas fixed his eyes on him. 'I should have had more damned sense! I'd worked it out by mathematics, but had never made a practical test . . . '

'These things happen sometimes,' Douglas muttered, without resentment. In fact he was rather surprised to find the physicist so penitent.

'I escaped the worst,' Brooks went on moodily. 'I ducked behind a machine and got nothing worse than deep cuts and a few abrasions. I'm told you're okay now; soon be about again. But . . . '

He stopped, fingering his lower lip.

'It isn't — Vera?' Douglas asked sharply, realizing that her name had not been mentioned so far. 'She wasn't — killed?'

'No — not that.' Brooks got to his feet under an uncontrollable agitation. 'She's alive — quite alive. In fact to look at her you wouldn't notice much difference. Face unmarked; body the same, only — You'd better see her,' he finished, as though he found the subject too much for him to handle alone.

He crossed to the door, opened it and reached outside. Douglas lay watching

20

fixedly as the girl was led into the room. As Brooks had said, she appeared no different — except for one thing. She was wearing large deep blue glass goggles and moving uncertainly, even though her brother held her arm.

Presently, as Douglas' horrified eyes bored at her, she reached the bedside. Her hands felt along the coverlet quickly, then she gave a little sigh of relief as Douglas' grip closed upon them.

Carefully Brooks guided her into the chair, then he stood looking down on her morosely.

'I'm glad you're all right, Doug,' she whispered, her voice hardly audible. 'I was so afraid you might die — '

'But you!' he cried. 'What in God's name — '

'She's blind!' Brooks said abruptly, and Vera's lips tightened at the brutal frankness of it. 'The explosion did it. Pieces of metal struck her in the eyes but missed her face. There was nothing for it but to remove the eyes entirely in case the metal fragments worked into the brain and caused death. Mercifully, her face is unscarred.'

'I'd sooner have died,' the girl muttered. 'What's the use of going on living in the dark? Why couldn't it have been anything else but this?' she burst out passionately. 'I wouldn't have minded losing an arm, or a leg: they can be replaced these days. But to me, to whom the whole essence of life lies in movement and change, to be condemned to blindness — '

Her voice stopped and the room was very quiet. Then she spoke again, with a half smile.

'Forget it,' she said. 'I'm all right now. Just gets me down when I think of it. I'm no quitter — but now and again I do got frightened of the blackness.'

Douglas stroked her slender hands gently, his eyes fixed on her.

'Would you mind taking the glasses off?' he asked quietly. 'I'm an oculist, remember.'

'I know, but even you can't repair what isn't there . . . ' The girl paused suddenly with a little catching of her breath. 'Or can you?' she whispered. 'I've just

22

remembered that you said something on that awful day about artificial eyes — '

'Take the glasses off,' Douglas insisted.

She fingered behind her ears and her brother turned away and looked through the window. What regard he had for his sister was revealed more in that action than in anything else.

Had he not been an oculist first and a lover second Douglas too would probably have looked away — but he didn't. He fixed his gaze on the empty, tightly closed eyelids where the girl's eyes had been. He studied the bluish spotting where metal fragments had been driven deep above her eyebrows and at the edges of her temples. Then, with an infinite delicacy, his finger-ends passed over the hollow eyelids . . . Finally he sat back.

'All right,' he said. 'Put them back.'

'Pretty dreadful, isn't it?' the girl sighed, adjusting the goggles back on the bridge of her nose.

Douglas did not answer for a moment. Presently he said slowly.

'I want you to take her home, Mason, and look after her well. I have to get myself right at the earliest possible moment, then I will tackle the problem exclusively. There may be a cure, in fact there has got to be! Vera can't go through the rest of her life in total darkness, not in this modern age.'

Brooks put a protecting arm round his sister's shoulders as she got up.

'What are you talking about?' he asked bluntly 'What's the use of raising false hopes? This isn't just eye trouble. The eyes themselves have gone!'

'But the sockets are undamaged,' Douglas answered. 'To put it more plainly, the scaffolding is still in good shape. I think I can create artificial eyes, and I've thought so for years. Now I have got to turn that thought into a fact!'

Brooks hesitated, then he gave an incredulous smile.

'Well, get yourself better anyway,' he said. 'Then we'll talk again. Come on, Vera — this way.'

Douglas clasped her hand again, then he watched as she was led from the room. He lay scowling for a while, then jabbed the bell push. From the nurse he ordered paper and pencil in such a fierce voice that she had inner fears for her safety.

The terrific stimulus of the tragedy he had witnessed got Douglas on his feet again in record time — and even before this he had spent every waking hour scribbling notes, making computations, testing theories, then discarding them. The first thing he did upon returning to his home was to catch up to date on his practice — which took him a fortnight — and then he closed down for a month for so-called health reasons.

This done he sent for Mason Brooks and Vera, summoning them to his surgery address, where he had better opportunity for using his equipment.

'I think this is a waste of time,' the physicist said briefly, after he had settled the girl in a chair. 'There's nothing you can do.'

'I insist that there is!' Douglas declared, pacing up and down. 'When I was in the nursing home I admit that I had my doubts; but I've worked out the final details since then. Just take a look at this . . . '

He switched on a floodlamp and motioned Brooks to a table directly under it. Delicately held in a platinum claw, adjustable by setscrews and pinions, was what appeared to be a human eyeball.

'Notice!' Douglas ordered, and switched the light off for a moment. Then when he flooded it on again the eye's artificial pupil contracted sharply.

'Hmm — pretty good,' the physicist admitted.

'It's damned good!' Douglas retorted. 'This eye is made primarily of mitonex plastic molded at two hundred F. That means it does not become solid and hard but retains the soft elasticity of the normal human eyeball. In front, of a different grade of mitonex and approaching the normal focusing curve of the human eye, is a plastic cornea, and behind it the lens itself. The iris was the easiest part. It's made on the principle of a camera iris, so delicately sprung that the action of light photons striking it cause it to contract. When light in excess ceases to strike it, it expands to the point considered normal. The iris itself contains pigment, as does the human eye . . . '

Douglas stopped for a moment and searched the scientist's lean, tensed face.

'I tell you, Mason, I've reproduced here everything the human eye possesses! A human being can be duplicated in any case; the body contains no chemicals that a laboratory cannot produce. By the same token I've reproduced an eye — the vitreous humor, the aqueous humor, the choroid coat, the sclerotic coat, everything.'

'Including the retina and optic nerve?' Brooks asked, still unconvinced.

'Including those! The retina is simply the spreading out of a mass of nerve fibers forming the optic nerve itself, at the back of the eye. The optic nerve is only a carrier of sensation, the same as an electric wire carries current. You can see it here — this fine golden thread with a copper core. This reproduces the optic nerve with all the details of the natural one. So you see, nothing is missing.'

'And you think it can give sight?' Brooks asked.

'I'm convinced of it!'

'Then I'm going to correct this dangerous illusion, much as I want Vera to have her sight back!' Brooks' face had become grim. 'You ought to know, even as a layman does, that the eye itself does not see! Put this in Vera's head and she'd still be stark blind!'

'If it were unconnected, yes,' Douglas agreed. 'But the power of sight is located in the cortex of the occipital lobe of the brain. The excitations there produced give rise to visual sensation. Connect the nerves of this artificial eye — or rather of both of them, since I have this eye in duplicate — to the right parts of the brain and vision is assured!'

The physicist became silent, the corners of his mouth dragged down. Vera got out of the chair and found her way to the table.

'This all sounds rather wonderful to me,' she said. 'I wish I could see this eye you're talking about.'

'The thing's too wonderful!' Brooks declared harshly. 'The very operation itself would be extremely dangerous. You admit that, Doug?'

'It would, yes,' he assented. 'But don't forget that I am an ophthalmic surgeon and have tackled similar difficult jobs — and succeeded. I believe I could succeed here, too, and if so, a new era in optics would be upon us.'

'If!' Brooks echoed. 'That implies a doubt! No, Douglas, you are not going to turn my sister into a guinea pig because of a bright idea you've got. I won't allow it!'

'You won't allow it!' Vera exclaimed. 'I've some say in this, remember. I'm the one who can't see — not you. I'm all for it. Anyway, if it fails, I'll be no worse off and I shall know where I stand.'

'I will not allow you to do it,' her brother insisted flatly. 'I've never yet made a decision on your behalf which proved wrong. And I say that this is too risky.'

'Don't you think you owe Vera a chance to get her sight back?' Douglas asked quietly. 'But for you and your experiment she wouldn't be blind anyway.'

The physicist tightened his lips.

'I'm of age, and I'm going to risk it,'

Vera decided finally. 'Name the day and the hour, Doug, and I'll be here — somehow.'

'If you do attempt this operation, Douglas, I'll bring the whole Ophthalmic Council down on your head,' Brooks declared. 'That isn't viciousness; it's plain commonsense. I know Vera is desperate, but I won't allow her to risk her life on an experiment that may prove fatal. In a year or two maybe perfection will be assured and other people will have taken the first blows — Certainly Vera won't! If the Ophthalmic Council get to know what you are doing, without their full sanction, it will mean you're sunk. You know that.'

Douglas drummed his fingers on the table, his face set.

'It's up to Vera, not you,' he said at length.

'Fix your day and let me know,' the girl answered.

'Vera, don't be such a little fool — !' Brooks gripped her arm.

'I'm not a fool! You don't know what I'm enduring! You are not wandering round in total darkness as I am. Do you

30

realize that it is nearly three months since I saw a ray of light? Groping for everything, bumping into things, unable to see how I look! I — I can't bear it much longer. I'd sooner die than stay blind. I'm going to take the risk, and be hanged to you!'

Brooks eyed her for a moment, then his jaw squared.

'We'll talk it over,' he decided, leading her to the door. 'And I'd advise you to think again, too, Douglas.'

'Sorry!' He opened the door. 'It's up to Vera.'

He kissed her gently and gripped her hand, then watched her and her brother go off down the corridor. Closing the door quietly he stood thinking, his face resolute.

3

Vision Beyond

At three o'clock that afternoon Douglas received a visiphone call from the Ophthalmic Council. It was the face of Dr. Grant Hurley, the Chairman, which appeared on the screen.

'The members have asked me to summon you to a meeting, Dr. Ashfield,' he stated impartially. 'A matter has come up which is — er — rather outside normal ethics in the matter of optics. The meeting will be an Extraordinary one and will be held at four this afternoon. You will make it convenient to be present, please.'

It was not a question but a statement.

'Of course, Doctor,' Douglas acknowledged, and switched off.

He had no illusions. Mason Brooks had evidently kept his word and tipped off the Council. By law they controlled all the oculists and ophthalmic surgeons in the city. One worked — with their permission — and stayed within their prescribed boundaries. Good in one way, for it stopped the inexperienced dabbler from injuring the public; but from Douglas Ashfield's point of view it was bad. Damned bad! Nor dare he refuse to attend a meeting if he wanted to remain in practice.

So at four o'clock he was in the Board Room with the seven directors of the Council and Chairman Hurley at the head of the long, shining table.

'Dr. Ashfield, I am in possession of a special letter sent to me this afternoon by Mr. Mason Brooks, the Chief Physicist with the City Scientists.' Dr. Hurley laid it on the table, open. 'Were it from a lesser member of the community I might have ignored its contents, so amazing are they, but from a man of Mr. Brooks' standing the matter at once assumes serious proportions. He declares that you are trying to persuade his sister, Miss Vera Brooks — recently blinded in an accident — to undergo an operation by which you can give her artificial eyes which can see!'

Douglas smiled bitterly at the pedantry of the man, the verbal groveling to a man worth millions of dollars.

'The allegation is correct, Doctor,' he answered briefly.

This started a hum of excited conversation round the table until Hurley's insistent, beating gavel silenced it.

'I can only presume, Dr. Ashfield, that you are joking,' Hurley said acidly. 'And I consider it most out of taste.'

'Gentlemen, I have created an artificial eye,' Douglas said, rather weary of having to repeat the details. 'It can do everything which a normal eye does. It can give sight to the blind and thereby advance optical science a century. It can remove the biggest blight, bar death, that threatens humanity!'

'It hasn't been done before,' said Wilson, reckoned as the best optic nerve man in the States.

'That's no criterion!' Douglas retorted, looking round on the incredulous faces. 'I'm not going to recall to your minds what men said about Watt with his steam engine, Bell and his telephone, Lister and his antiseptic. I think you are intelligent men, willing to listen to anything that means advancement. I can provide it — and prove it.'

'Since you can prove it, we are willing to listen,' Dr. Hurley answered expansively. 'How soon can you produce this — proof?'

'The moment I have operated on Vera Brooks.'

'This is becoming a vicious circle,' Hurley decided, ominous again. 'We cannot permit an operation on a woman — and especially one so high in the social scale — without the method and result being thoroughly considered beforehand. We, the Council as a whole, forbid such an operation without proof first!'

Douglas gestured impatiently. 'How in the world can I prove it until a human being has had the benefit?' he demanded. 'To try it on an animal would not convince you. An animal cannot tell us if it can see properly, even though we can discover if it reacts as though it can. I well know that the Council always needs sweeping proof — beyond a shadow of doubt. And the only way I can get it is by performing an operation — on a human being — on Vera Brooks!'

There was a silence, then the Chairman cleared his throat noisily.

'If you could perhaps find somebody less important?' he suggested. 'After all, the financial resources of Miss Brooks and her brother have a great deal to do with the welfare of the city as a whole!'

'If, as you suggest, I were to use these artificial eyes on a beggar, it would take me ten years to make another pair!' Douglas retorted. 'Do you imagine I would leave Miss Brooks, my future wife, in her present condition that long? No, gentlemen! In any case she has given her own personal sanction to the operation.'

'Prompted by the elusive hope of regained sight, no doubt,' Dr. Hurley said pompously. 'I am sorry, Dr. Ashfield. Either you operate on someone unknown — and a volunteer, of course — and show the results, or we cannot be interested. If, in spite of everything, you proceed with an operation on Miss Brooks, you will be precluded forthwith from practicing, and that, I am afraid, would terminate the career of a very clever ophthalmic surgeon.'

'If even Miss Brooks herself asked you to let me do it?' Douglas asked despairingly.

'Even then,' Hurley replied adamantly. 'Miss Brooks is in no position to make a decision. She is a drowning woman clutching at a straw. In matters medical it is the Council, not the individual, who makes the decisions these days. That is the law, you know.'

Douglas hesitated for a moment, his bitter eyes glaring at the stony faces. Then, without a word, he pushed his chair back under the table and left the room.

Ten minutes later the visiphone was ringing in the Brooks' re-built residence, and the manservant answered. After a while Vera's face with dark glasses appeared on the viewplate.

'Vera? Doug speaking . . . I'm going to operate. Your brother has done his damnedest with the Ophthalmic Council and they'll disown me for it. I'm risking that . . . if you'll risk your life?'

'Doug, you know I will. I believe in you — always shall. I meant it when I told you to name the day.'

'All right, then — this evening. I have two expert nurses I can call upon. I'll perform the operation in my own surgery. All I want you to do is go without food from now on. Can't undergo an operation on a full stomach — I'll call to see you on the pretext of taking you for a drive, then Mason won't suspect — I hope.'

'I think he'll be out anyway,' the girl responded. 'He's hard at work in the city laboratory after hours trying to reshape that idea of his which got us in this mess . . . When it's over, Doug, the Ophthalmic Council will just have to believe!'

'Yes . . . ' Douglas had a mental vision of Hurley's beefy, pompous face. 'Perhaps. Anyway, I'll be with you at seven this evening.'

'Seven it is,' Vera agreed, and switched off.

Promptly at seven Douglas was at the Brooks residence — and as the girl had anticipated, her brother was absent, and probably would be until a late hour.

Douglas helped her into the car, then, driving it himself, he threaded his way through the city streets towards his own suite in the Cosmopolitan Building.

'Cheerful?' he murmured, as the girl sat beside him.

'More than I've ever been since I became blind,' she replied. 'At first it seemed that there was no way out. I'd forgotten all about that talk we had at the Golden Comet about artificial eyes. But now — Oh, I know you'll succeed!'

'I've got to,' he said grimly. 'Not only because you are the most precious possession I have, not only because I want you to be a happy, carefree girl again — but because of what success will mean to humanity in general. But you must understand, dearest, that there is the risk of failure. I have to be fair with you on that point. In any event Mason will no doubt kill me if I fail; I'm sure of that.'

'I'll take my chance,' she answered quietly; then she added rather plaintively, 'I suppose I can't have something to eat? My sides are nearly touching.'

'All the better, and you can't have a bite,' Douglas said firmly. 'I'm a surgeon now, not your fiancé . . . Well, here we are . . . '

He ran the car into the big private garage, then helped the girl out and guided her fumbling feet up the steps and so through the hall to the elevator. Once in his office he took her straight through to the surgery and settled her down in a chair. The two nurses he had summoned caught his nod and one of them began to remove the girl's hat and coat.

While they prepared her for the operation he went into his private office and stood for a moment with his fists clenched and his eyes tightly shut.

'All I ask is the strength of my hands, the infallibility of my instruments, and the judgment of posterity,' he breathed. 'Grant me that . . . no more.'

His brief prayer over, he straightened up and went back into the surgery. While he washed his hands and snapped on rubber gloves, the girl sank into unconsciousness under the anesthetic. He came to the table at last, stood looking down on

40

the eyeless sockets, at the shaven scalp — then he took the instrument the leading nurse handed to him, and began.

For an hour he labored — for two hours, struggling under the hot glare of the shadowless lamps. Now and again as he worked he caught the astonished eyes of the nurses above their facemasks as they saw him insert and connect the artificial eyes. He could see they were incredulous. The eyeballs themselves he never touched. The platinum claws did the work, handling them as gently as if they were thistledown. Little by little he progressed, knitting the optic nerve to the appropriate portion of the brain, making new nerve connections, re-knitting the blood vessels.

In two hours he was feeling tired — but the work was done. The girl's skull had been re-stitched and the scar coated in fast healing astringents. She lay now in the soft airbed adjoining the surgery, a bandage around her head and eyes.

When he felt fit enough after his labors — towards two in the morning — Douglas crept in to look at her. The nurse was nodding in the chair by her side. The girl was breathing regularly; her temperature and pulse were normal. Douglas gave the nurse a nudge and then went out again to his private office to sit down and await the dawn.

This time it was the nurse who awakened him. He got into his coat hurriedly and walked through to the bedroom. The girl was fully conscious again, and apparently in good spirits.

'Doug?' she asked quickly, recognizing his footsteps. 'How am I getting on? I still can't see anything.'

'You're not supposed to, dearest.' He gripped her hands. 'You are all bandaged up. But you're doing fine. Think yourself lucky you didn't live in an earlier medical era, or this operation would have taken months of convalescence. Surgery has upped a bit since the old days . . . How's your appetite?'

'Last night my sides were touching — now they've stuck together! Do something, please!'

'Okay. Nurse!'

The woman came in and Douglas gave

his orders. Then he turned back to the girl. 'While you have your meal I'll freshen up a bit — then we'll see how things are. You should be able to stand it then.'

'It'll be all right, Doug; I know it will!'

He patted her hand and left her. He had hardly reached his office preparatory to getting a shave, when he heard the door of the reception office being thumped good and hard. He went out to it and found Mason Brooks on the threshold, his face white with ill-controlled fury.

'Where's Vera?' he blazed, striding in. 'She's here?'

'Yes, she's here,' Douglas assented quietly, shutting the door. 'And take it easy.'

'Easy! That's a fine thing to tell me! I've been at work all night and I arrive home to find my sister has been absent all that time — never been seen since you called for her last evening in your car. What the hell have you been doing? Where is she?'

'Having her breakfast at the moment

— and there's a nurse with her, and has been all night.'

Douglas took off his coat leisurely and turned to the mirror. He had just picked up the electric razor when Brooks caught his arm and whirled him round.

'You can't treat this matter as of no consequence, Doug!' he snapped, his eyes glittering. 'You're hoping to make that experiment on Vera, in spite of all I've done to try and stop you — '

'And in spite of your very ungallant efforts with the Ophthalmic Council!' Douglas retorted. 'I'm not making the experiment, Mason; I've *made* it! I performed the operation last night and Vera still lives, and is well.'

The physicist perspired visibly in sudden relief. He sank into a nearby chair. Then he passed a hand over his smooth dark head.

'I'm — I'm sorry,' he said agitatedly. 'I got all worked up. It — it was for Vera's sake, of course . . . '

'Of course.' Douglas ran the razor down his jaw.

'Can she — see?' Brooks questioned abruptly.

'That I don't know yet, but we'll find out when she's had her breakfast.'

There was silence between them for a while. Douglas finished his shaving and washing as the scientist thought things out.

'Better get a grip on yourself,' Douglas suggested, half smiling. 'Let's see how things are, shall we?'

'Yes. Yes, of course.'

Mason Brooks went into the girl's room beside him. He stood looking at his sister fixedly, but said no word. Since he evidently did not wish to intimate his presence, Douglas did not do it for him. He dismissed the nurse, then took hold of the girl's hand tightly.

'It's zero hour, Vera,' he said tensely. 'Are you ready?'

'Yes . . . ' Her voice was subdued. 'I'm ready.'

He reached behind her head, unfastened the clip to the eye bandage and began to unravel it. As the last shred fell away Brooks could not help a little gasp of amazement at the sight of the beautiful eyes in the formerly dead sockets. They were big and gray, even prettier than the girl's own had been.

There was a long, deadly silence. Douglas could feel himself perspiring freely under the suspense. Brooks leaned very slightly forward, his eyes sharpened to needle points.

Slowly the girl turned her bandaged head. She looked above to either side of her — then she fixed her eyes wonderingly on Douglas. He stared back fixedly — but to his astonishment she clapped her hands to her face.

'What?' he asked desperately, catching her shoulder. 'Vera, what is it? What's wrong? Can't you see? You *must*, I tell you!'

'Yes — yes, I can see,' she answered breathlessly, lowering her hands again. 'I can see you — and Mace over there — and this room. I can see myself . . . But — but *I can see two things at once*! Nothing looks solid any more! I can see through the walls. There is a crazy looking landscape out there, weirdly vast. And

some ruins of some sort — like cities
. . . It's — it's *awful*!'

She covered her eyes again and
Douglas stood looking at her in bewilder-
ment.

'Brain reaction maybe,' he muttered.
'Hallucinations.'

'More likely you've damaged her
brain!' Brooks declared hotly, crossing the
room. 'Two things at once, man! Do you
realize?'

He caught Douglas' arm. The way the
two men looked at each other was a
prelude to blows — but the girl's voice
stopped them.

'Fighting over it isn't going to do any
good — and certainly not to me. Try
behaving yourselves instead! Come here,
both of you.'

They hesitated a moment, then came
to the bedside. Vera had lost that
expression of alarm now and instead was
looking more puzzled than anything else.

'At least I can see,' she decided. 'That
is something for which I shall be eternally
grateful, Doug — but you've got to do
something about this double vision if you

can. Maybe you made a mistake in the lenses. After, all, it was your first attempt.'

'Yes, it's possible,' he admitted.

'Just what are your impressions?' Brooks asked, his anger cooling into interest. 'Explain them in detail.'

'Well, I can see as far as the walls of this room — then beyond them I can see New York spread out on all sides, but in the midst of it — like a double exposure photograph — is some kind of landscape. It's deserted and seems to go on forever and forever. Same with the sky, too. No horizon. Endless — utterly endless.'

The girl looked up at the ceiling, then jerked her eyes back again and blinked.

'The sun's up there — but it looks different. It's got curly things flickering round its edges and there's a blaze of white light behind it.'

'Great Scott, the solar prominences and corona!' Brooks whispered incredulously. 'Well — go on!'

'I can see through my own body,' the girl went on, 'but not into it, if you understand. And although I can see through these immediate walls, I cannot see through more distant ones . . . Yes, I can see through the floor, down through this building, into the underground railway and sewage system, then deep down into the earth. Like lying in mid-air over a colossal pit!'

Mason Brooks scowled in deep thought. First and foremost a physicist, the girl's impressions had arrested something in his mind. To Douglas, purely an oculist, the matter was alarming.

'We can't leave things like this,' he decided. 'Rest until this afternoon, Vera, and then you'll be fit to get up and dress. First thing I'll do is get you into the surgery and make an examination. Obviously you've got X-ray eyes and shouldn't have. I must have made a mistake somewhere in those lenses.'

The girl closed her eyes and gave a serene smile.

'There, that's better. Now I can't see anything at all.'

'Did you say something about cities? Ruins?' her brother asked presently.

She opened her eyes again and regarded him queerly. It was a rather unnerving stare she gave him, a perfect example of looking straight through him.

'Yes, I did,' she assented. 'They're behind you. It's mixed up with New York's buildings somehow. But there are ruins on a sort of rough plain.'

'Hum!' Brooks said, and patted her shoulder. 'Okay, you just close your eyes and take it easy. We'll discuss this later. And don't say anything to the nurse, either. You may have acquired a gift!'

The girl shrugged and closed her eyes again. Douglas gave her a final puzzled look and then followed Brooks from the room. The nurse went in and took over her duties again.

In the reception office the physicist rubbed his unshaven jaw thoughtfully.

'You're a man of optics, Douglas. What's your verdict?'

'I must have made an error in the formula somewhere — or else synthetic material doesn't react like normal tissue. That's the only explanation. Given time I could probably right it. Or even the use of spectacles might cut out that distant superimposing wavelength.'

Brooks gave a grim smile.

'I've other ideas! I'm beginning to think that you have all unwittingly unlocked a closed door. My sister isn't looking through things, but into things! If she could see through things, in the fashion of X-rays, she would simply see all New York and the ground as though it were glass. But she doesn't. Only at very short focus can she penetrate a wall — and beyond that she sees an entire second landscape. Broken down cities, solar prominences and corona, a sky and plain that go on forever in a straight line. To me, as a physicist, that hints at only one thing — *the fourth dimension*!'

'What!' Douglas yelped. 'You're crazy, man!'

'Mebbe,' Brooks shrugged. 'But remember that the greatest discoveries of science are often the outcome of the sheerest accident. It's only a theory yet — and I've got to think about it.' He glanced at his watch. 'I'm going home for breakfast and a freshen up. I'll be back here this afternoon and we'll go into the thing properly.'

He strode to the doorway, then

51

half-way through it he paused and looked back.

'Sorry I blew up.' He grinned cynically. 'Maybe this will have justified your work, after all.'

4

Dimensional Possibilities

By mid-afternoon the girl was quite able to be up and about. Douglas' examination satisfied him that the most modern of restoratives had done their work and that except for her peculiar eye trouble and the wig she was wearing until her hair grew again she was about normal.

At three o'clock Brooks arrived, as immaculate and keen as if attending a science convention. And from the expression on his leanly cut face he had been doing a good deal of thinking.

The girl herself was in difficulties, so she said. She seemed half afraid to walk about for fear she would fall through the floor, and as she moved she dodged invisible objects at times. To the two men watching the effect was serio-comic.

'We'll see what's wrong anyway,' Douglas decided, leading the way into the surgery. 'Take a seat, Vera.'

She sat down in the padded chair amidst the optical instruments and her brother stood with his hands in his trouser pockets, studying her. Douglas drew up the big ophthalmoscope and then switched off the lights.

'While we are in the dark, and before I start to examine you, what do you see?' he asked.

'I'm not in the dark,' she answered surprisingly. 'I can see a sunlit plain all round me, very clearly within the square which is this darkened room — but beyond it, where the sun is shining on New York, the vision is doubled, of course.'

'This gets better as it goes on,' Douglas muttered.

He switched on the minute probing beam of the ophthalmoscope and the spot of light settled on the girl's left pupil. Through the testing lens Douglas peered deep into the artificial eyes he had created, at the redness of the retina at the back, at the edges of the artificial pupil. He did the same for the other eye, increasing the light power until the girl complained that he was hurting her. Then he switched off and drew back the window shades.

'Every reaction perfect!' he declared, baffled. 'There is not the least reason why you should see two things at once! Everything ought to be normal!'

'I'm sorry — but it just isn't,' she shrugged.

'And I'll tell you why,' her brother said slowly. 'I think, Doug, that the fault lies in the artificial cornea you've made — the front surface of the eye. Any oculist knows — or a layman too, for that matter — that a fault in this clear membrane can produce queer effects. The most common is astigmatism. If the cornea is curved in different directions, the rays of light in different meridians can't be brought into focus on the retina except by an irregular strain on the muscles. Objects therefore look distorted and out of place. Now in this case you have an artificial cornea that might quite easily be several degrees out of true focus. The effect is not just a distortion, but an ability to collect light waves which no normal human eye can see! In a way, you have provided Vera with a sixth sense. X-ray eyesight exists in some people — and they are usually on the stage or in sideshows — but this is something more! Something wonderful! It is the recovery of a sense we must all have possessed at some time in the past.'

'How do you make that out?' Douglas demanded.

'By the fact that a human brain can still work unharmed with eyes like this attached to it. Since it does not cause any pain or damage, it proves it is a sense which is not — er — unaccustomed.'

'All this talking may be interesting to you two experimenters,' Vera objected, 'but I'm still living in a double exposure world! I want it put right!'

'Let me finish, Sis,' her brother insisted, going over to her. 'I've been thinking about this business — thinking hard. Tell me something — as you move about does your vision of this other world alter too? As though you'd covered a certain distance in it?'

'Yes. I seem to cover the same distance

there as I do here.'

'Good! That means that that other world actually exists and is not just a figment of the mind. I believe that you are looking into nothing else but the fourth dimension! Remember that I have studied these things — planes of existence, inter-atomic spaces, and so forth.'

'Fourth dimension!' Vera exclaimed, startled. 'Good Lord! But — but that's Time, isn't it? Or am I wrong?'

'The fourth dimension is not Time,' Brooks assured her, shaking his sleek head. 'In fact nobody knows exactly what it is, although there are numerous theories. As explained in geometry, it is an infinite extension in length and breadth whereby both states are unbounded. There are no curves, as we see them. Eddington described it as Past, Present, Future, and *Elsewhere*. Think of it this way. A bus is moving at twenty-five miles an hour, forwards — A man is going to the upper deck of that bus — *upwards*, while the bus is going forward. Four states are involved. The man goes upward and forward simultaneously at differing ratios of speed — yet both occupy the same instant in time and space. That's an everyday conception of the fourth dimension.'

'Then it's too much for me!' Vera declared flatly.

'Well, it's not surprising,' Brooks shrugged. 'Anyway, this land you see must lie right in this very space we occupy, but nobody has ever seen it before because they have not had the eyes with which to do it. It is not an impossible thing. Matter, as we know it, is mainly composed of empty space. Unless we accept that Nature is incredibly wasteful with her material, we have to admit that there must be other planes — or one other plane, the fourth dimension — lying in the empty space between. That is, in the space interstices between atomic systems. From what you can see I begin to think the matter is no longer in doubt . . . '

'Then where does all this get us?' Douglas asked.

'We may be at the beginning of an amazing trail,' Brooks replied slowly. 'For years I have experimented with solids into solids, as you know — and now, because of a fluke in these artificial eyes, you've given this scatter-brained sister of mine the power to see into the very spaces which I have tried to penetrate! From, now on our journey is into pure science.'

'Then — then don't I get my eyes put right?' the girl asked anxiously.

'Not until you have been of immeasurable service, anyway,' Brooks answered. 'You've been a pretty useless member of the community up to now, but here's your supreme chance to advance science!' He took her arm as she got up from the chair. 'Now, you spoke of a ruined city. How far away is it?' She turned and looked towards the door side of the surgery wall.

'Over there, about two miles. Why?'

'You are going there to examine it.'

'Oh! How?'

'I'll show you. Come on.'

She put on her hat and coat and between both men was led downstairs and into the street. Here, amidst the people on the sidewalk and the swirl and bluster of traffic she drew back nervously.

'I — I daren't go forward!' she insisted,

frightened. 'It's all too horribly confus-
ing!'

'You're all right,' her brother told her
calmly. 'Close your eyes if you can't stick
it. Now, where are the ruins?'

'Behind that stereo-theatre over there.'

'Good! Shut your eyes and hang on!'

Thuswise she was escorted across the
street until they came behind the
stereo-theatre. Here was a stretch of
wasteland under option for future building.

'How now?' Brooks asked eagerly.

The girl looked about her. 'Much
nearer,' she announced. 'We are apparently floating half way up a small hillside
and the city is a bit further on, on the flat
plain at the top of the hill — that way.'

They followed the direction she gave
and finished up in one of New York's
expansive parks. Here there were open
grounds and trees aplenty.

'I'm amidst the ruins now,' the girl
said, as she looked round on the trees and
the distant reclining people on seats.
'There are the remains of buildings here,
crumbled into masonry.'

'Can you touch this masonry?' Brooks asked, thinking.

She waved a hand in the air before her. 'No. My hand goes through it.'

'Then that shows you are still in three dimensions as much as Doug and I are. We are standing on *this* ground in this plane: that is why, to you, we seem to float in mid-air on the other side. Okay, you see ruined buildings: anything else?'

'It all seems to go for such a long way,' the girl replied, awe-stricken. 'Endless expanse! These city ruins extend over a tremendous distance — nearly as much as New York itself. It might take me months to explore it all. And remember that I can't go through walls, or doors. Though I can see the outside of ruins, I cannot see into them, unless one wall be down.'

'I realize that,' Brooks nodded. 'Anyway, you have come across some immense scientific secret of which we have never known, and which no other person but you can even see. What we do now is keep beside you while you explore. If you find anything at all important, describe it in detail.'

Vera nodded, rather mystified, and

walked forward. And it was the beginning of daily visits to the park. By degrees Vera forced herself to become accustomed to her disturbing, visual sight and finally was able to move about, when necessary without an escort. To the outer world, and the Press — for the newspapers were hot on her track — she pretended to be half blind and slowly recovering from an operation. Those were her brother's orders, and they certainly killed Douglas Ashfield's practice stone dead. The Ophthalmic Council struck him forthwith off the register . . . But he was not embittered: the wonder of the thing he had fortuitously created fascinated him . . .

Every dinnertime, every afternoon, or in the light evenings, Vera walked in the park with her brother and Douglas, always in some different area of it. The beauty of it was that nobody knew what they were up to. It simply looked, to keen newshounds, as though the unfortunate blind heiress was taking her usual constitutional.

Then, three months later, in which

time the girl had about covered every foot of that enormous, deserted other-world city, she made a discovery. Amidst the crumbled walls of one huge building were machines, so perfectly made and of such indestructible material that they were still useable — if only they could be reached.

'Describe them,' Brooks insisted, when he first heard her mention the machines. 'In absolute detail. I'll fit in the parts you don't understand.'

So Vera did her best. She was by no means lucid, being utterly ignorant of science in general and machinery in particular. But by interrogating her closely and insisting on the smallest intricacy, her brother built up over the weeks an exact outline of the particular machine she was describing.

Through the autumn and winter they were on the job, to the occasional surprise of the newshounds, and at length when the following spring came, Brooks decided that the walks were no longer necessary. In his own laboratory, rebuilt in its entirety after the disaster of the preceding year, he explained why.

'I think it may be possible to enter this plane, this fourth dimension, with our physical bodies,' he said. 'Then we can see for ourselves just what is going on.'

'Sounds like a big assumption to me,' Douglas commented.

'And even if we could go there, there is nothing to see,' Vera said with a shrug. 'I've told you it's flat and uninteresting, with a lot of scattered ruins.'

'Listen to me,' the scientist's sharp voice interrupted her. 'You have described to me machines which could only have been made by a master race. The very nature of the machines and the invulnerable atomic structure comprising them proves that. If — as seems likely — a master race lived and died in a plane so close to us, it is essential to science that we find out everything about them.

'You have been very helpful in describing the machines to me, and one of them — which I made you concentrate on exclusively — is undoubtedly electronic in basis. I've worked out the details from the facts you gave me and have reproduced the machine here. Take a look at it. Is it like the one you described?'

The girl studied it, wishing there was not that irritating background of land and crazy sky surrounding it.

'Near as I can remember it, yes,' she assented.

'Good! Now I'll tell you what it is. It's very similar to my own conception of matter-into-matter, only it possesses many refinements borrowed from that otherworld design. With my knowledge of my own invention, helped by the essential details of this one, I've produced a device that should carry us into that plane. Here is how:

'Between us and it, there exists only one barrier, that of vibration. If it were a solid barrier, light waves could not pass through it and Vera would not be able to see the things she does. So, since we cannot touch anything in that plane while we are in this one, it shows that our bodies — and the material things about us — are not attuned to the same rate of vibration. Anybody knows that we can only encounter things on our own scale of vibration, just the same as we can only

65

hear things in a certain range of wave-length.'

The scientist took a deep breath and smiled at them.

'This machine, duplicated from the one Vera has described, alters the vibration of the body. It should, as I see it, cause us to fade from sight in this three-dimensioned world and become attuned instead to the vibrations of the other one, just as a piece of ice melts from one form of solidity and partakes of the molecular state of water. Do you understand?'

'I think I do,' Douglas answered. 'But it seems to involve a high degree of risk.'

'I don't think so,' Brooks answered. 'This time it is not a case of a solid into a solid, but of three solids into comparatively thin air. Certainly I am going to risk it, and I'm hoping you two will do likewise.'

'Now?' the girl asked, startled.

'Well, say tomorrow morning. That will give us the rest of today to tidy up our business affairs and have a good night's rest. I have a vacation due me, so I can manage it.'

'And my time's my own since my practice went to the bad,' Douglas sighed.

Vera was silent. Brooks' face grew impatient.

'Confound it all, what is there to hesitate at in such an opportunity?' he demanded. 'We're going to attempt something nobody ever attempted before. It's science that must progress, no matter what our puny bodies suffer in consequence. It won't be dangerous. Just unusual.'

'Unusual is right!' Vera murmured. She shrugged. 'All right, I'll risk it. I've played with death many a time in my personal aircraft, so this may be something new. How about you, Doug?'

'You don't think I'm going to lose my hold on you?' he said with a smile. 'I'm staying beside you until your eyes can be put right and we can be married. Incidentally I'm working on that eye formula. I intend to find what produced the flaw, no matter what happens.'

'The flaw mustn't be corrected yet,' Brooks said. 'Well, you'll come?'

'Tomorrow morning it is,' Douglas agreed

5

Wonderland

Promptly at ten the following morning, their various affairs in order for an indefinite time, the three met again in Brooks' laboratory. He was looking as alert as usual, full of confidence that his experiment would be successful.

'Just one thing I should mention,' he said, as he switched on the dynamos. 'This machine will keep us in that other plane as long as the vibratory effect lasts. That is to say, the moment we arrive there our vibratory rate will start to slow down imperceptibly as the atoms change their set-up in our bodies. The effect of the machine upon us will not be a permanent state. Like a charged battery we'll being running down, and when the effect has altogether faded — when the electric change of atoms has reverted to normal — we'll find ourselves back in our own plane here. As near as I can calculate, it should be two or three hours before we return.'

'Suppose we snap back under a lake or a truck?' Vera asked.

'With your eyes to see in two places at once? I think not. You'll be our infallible guide.'

'Suppose I lose my dual vision when I get there?'

'I don't think that'll happen,' Brooks answered. 'We'll soon see, anyhow. As for other details — here are three packs of provisions and small arms. Put one each on your backs. Finally, I have locked the laboratory door and nobody can enter until summoned by me. That makes us safe. Now — are you ready?'

The girl and Douglas nodded. Stepping into the metal-plated area of the machine, directly under two long bar-magnets, they watched the next procedure. Brooks joined them and reached out to a switch. Immediately the power from the magnetic devices overhead made itself felt. Not painful exactly, but more like a tremendous stretching and elongation.

Before the eyes of both men, the laboratory began to shift crazily and seemed smeared in spirals and circles of black. To the girl no such evidence was present, but she could feel an intense dizziness trying to overcome her. Gazing as she was into two places simultaneously, and with an apparent void now yawning under her feet, the effect was nearly unbearable.

Then, for the two men at least, there came a feeling of enormous buoyancy. At the same instant the laboratory snuffed out like a candle flame and they felt themselves reeling backwards.

Darkness. Then a blaze of light.

It took Douglas several seconds to realize that he was lying flat on his back on hard ground, staring up at a dull blue sky in which stars and sun sailed together.

And what a sun!

Apart from its heat and brilliance, it was oddly crazy. It bulged forwards somehow — a flaming oval instead of a circle, edged with flaring, twisting prominences while, behind it into space, streamed the ghostly beauty of the corona.

Slowly he got up, dazzled by his glimpse of the orb of day. He slipped a hand under Vera's arm and helped her rise too. Brooks raised himself to his knees, gazed round, then straightened slowly to his feet.

'Apparently we did it,' Douglas observed, in an awe-struck voice.

The physicist didn't answer. For the moment he was as astounded as Douglas by the sight of this strange land into which they had come.

They were standing on a flat and dusty plain cracked here and there in irregular lines as though moisture was the very rarest occurrence. The plain, broken at intervals by a low-lying range of hills, just went on and on until it was lost in incredible distance.

There was a horizon, perhaps. But it was so remotely far away — a mere smudge joined by the deep blue sky — that the flat sky and the earth never did seem to meet. In every direction this condition was the same and, so far as the two men were concerned, there was not the vaguest suggestion of the three-dimensional plane from which they had come.

In the immediate foreground were the city ruins the girl had mentioned, showing their presence by the shells of once superb buildings, broken columns of stone, cracked and crumbling terraces. It had been very lovely here — once.

The air was windless and warm. In fact there did not seem to be any atmospheric disturbance at all. A silence reigned, a silence so overwhelming that it filled them with vague fears. Not a cry of a bird, the rumble of traffic from any city, or the roar of a waterfall came to their ears. Just the deadly all-embracing calm prevailed there, in the glare of that preposterous sun. It made all three feel strangely insignificant.

Brooks found his voice at last and turned to his sister.

'How's your vision now?'

'Just as it was,' she answered. 'The only difference now is that New York is super-imposed on top of this, instead of things being the other way round. We are standing in a space just outside the laboratory, by the way.'

Brooks shaded his eyes and glanced at the sun. Again he surveyed the infinity of landscape.

'Definitely the fourth dimension!' he decided at length. 'It explains much. Science has always believed that we humans had a precious tiny segment of Earth upon which to live considering our prolificacy.'

'I've read about the fourth dimension, of course, but things here don't seem to match up,' Douglas remarked, thinking. 'I've always thought we ought to be able to see around corners, experience wonderful changes in Time, and so on. All we can see is a rather fantastic interpretation of three dimensions.'

'That's to be expected,' the physicist answered laconically. 'We are not four-dimensional people, don't forget! Embedded in our brains is a long heritage of three-dimensional surroundings. Unless we achieve four-dimensional sight and senses to match, the only changes apparent to us are the infinite extension of length, this landscape, and the removal of certain flaws in light waves. If we were really four-dimensional

we would no doubt see many other wonders.'

Brooks glanced at his watch and
Douglas and the girl looked at theirs.

'How about taking a proper look at
those machines I saw?' Vera suggested. 'I
can take you straight to them.'

Brooks was about to answer when
Douglas suddenly called attention to a
curious phenomenon eastwards.

'I may be wrong,' he said, studying it,
'but it looks to me as though part of the
landscape has dropped out!'

Brooks stared also. Because of her
double vision Vera did not concentrate on
the task. Finally her brother nodded.

'Something queer all right,' he agreed.
'But it isn't a piece missing out of the
landscape. It's water! A sea! Stretching
away right to infinity and reflecting the
stars so perfectly it looks as though the
very nature of things has dropped away.
The dividing line between sea and sky
can't be detected. Come on. Let's
examine it now and view the machines
later.'

They began to move towards it — and

received their first four-dimensional shock. In five minutes, though the sea had appeared to be at least twenty miles away, they had reached its shore! The smallest of wavelets lapped on the silent, dusty sand, which in turn joined up with the dry, cracked landscape.

'Tidal, anyway,' Brooks commented, staring along the shoreline. 'See the mark where it reached last time?'

'It's something to hear a sound other than ourselves,' Vera whispered. 'There's something about this great, empty, infinite land which is terrifying. It's alien. Weird!'

'What puzzles me is how the devil we covered such a distance in five minutes,' Douglas observed, frowning. 'Vera, you can judge how far we've moved by being able to see New York. What distance would you say we've covered from our starting point?'

'About a mile. But in this place it did look like twenty.'

'Only one of the many things we may find odd here,' Brooks reflected. 'Light waves are probably responsible. Distance in our own plane is judged by light waves, of course, and in three dimensions at least, their velocity is fixed at one hundred and eighty-six thousand miles a second.

'Go faster than that and according to Fitzgerald's Contraction a minus quantity is produced. Here, apparently, light waves move far faster than that. It is conceded by science that light waves might have no fixed velocity when operating in four dimensions, and the same law applies to the critical speed of matter.

'Anyway we are here, having literally covered twenty miles in five minutes. Inertia, speed, space, Time — they're all haywire in this place.'

He became silent again and the unearthly calm returned, broken only by the suck of waves in the flowing tide. The sun had moved visibly across the deep blue heaven since they had arrived and was still traveling westwards. After a while Vera gave a sudden cry and pointed towards a spot apparently two miles away.

'Is it the sunlight, my eyes, or am I just

76

plain crazy?' she asked. 'Can that be the hulk of a ship?'

The two men turned, startled at such an implication. But it was not the girl's double vision playing her false. There was something there, catching the sun's rays. It looked like rotten timbers and the masts of a wrecked schooner.

'This is worth looking at,' Douglas exclaimed. 'Come on.'

He hurried forward and, to the amazement of Brooks and the girl a yard or two behind him, he became, apparently, remote in a couple of strides. When they finally caught up with him he was beside the wreck. They had to pull up short to save bumping into him.

'Going to take us a bit of time to get used to this light wave variation,' Brooks said. He stopped talking as his interest centered in the half-buried ship.

Obviously it had been here for many years — but the apparent lack of elemental fury in this dimension had prevented it from losing much of its original form. Stout timbers were still recognizable, though warped in places

77

from their nails. The masts had collapsed half across the deck amidst chipped and rotting canvas sails. The entire ship lay on her side, half of her mast buried in the sand.

'*Kobenhavn*,' Vera said, shading her eyes and peering up at the prow. 'I can just make it out, if it means anything.'

'Queer name,' Douglas answered, prowling in the sand and peering at the age-old timbers. 'This ship's pretty ancient, too. A four-masted schooner, I'd say. They went out of fashion ages ago. But how the devil did it ever get into this plane?'

He turned, his question aimed at Brooks. But to his surprise the physicist had joined Vera and was staring up at the nearly obliterated name on the bows. Gradually an astounded expression came over his face.

'The *Kobenhavn*! Of course!' He snapped his fingers. 'It's Danish, one of the famous missing ships on Lloyd's list! What were the facts now?'

He frowned as he reflected, staring at the sand.

'I once read an account of famous

missing ships, and as near as I can recall she was last seen close to the island of Tristan da Cunha on January twenty-first, Nineteen twenty-nine. It was seen by the people of that island. After that she was never heard of again and there were no storms or accidents to account for her disappearance. She just vanished.'

'And turned up here?' Vera asked incredulously. 'It's impossible!'

'It's not impossible because it's here,' Brooks replied, with cold logic. 'Say, this begins to open a field. There are lots of missing ships in the archives of Lloyd's — the *Cyclops*, the *Eltham*, the mystery of the *Marie Celeste* crew, never satisfactorily cleared up.

'Then we have vanished airplanes which have gone into the unknown when over oceans. Amelia Earhart, for instance. Then there have been ghost ships at sea where one ship has passed through another if we are to believe the famous legend of the Flying Dutchman. That effect could be produced by the mariners of the third dimension somehow being able to see a ship floating on a sea in the fourth dimension — this sea perhaps. I must think this out carefully.'

'We might find something yet remaining in the cabins of this wreck,' Douglas suggested. 'The ship's in fair order despite some several decades of time ravage. Let's take a look.'

Brooks nodded promptly and Douglas led the way carefully up the creaking, and in places rotten timbers. They had no easy job, but finally they did reach the sloping deck. Vera climbed up behind them and they assisted her along the steeply slanting surface to the nearest companionway.

The steps had practically rotted away and the door at the bottom was missing. By dint of lowering themselves carefully they got down without mishap and, as they had guessed, found themselves in the captain's cabin.

It was untidy, the captain's cabin, but nothing more than that. The grand old seasoned timbers had withstood the test of years well. The cabin would have been orderly if it had been upright. As it was, the table lay overturned in a corner. The drawers had spewed from a rack in the wall while cupboard doors had flown open. The most natural thing of all was a still untarnished brass hurricane lamp standing upright in its universal socket.

'This is uncanny!' Vera breathed, breaking the dreadful silence. 'I feel as though we're exploring beyond death!'

'Put that way, we are,' Brooks shrugged, scientific as ever. 'No time to be squeamish. There ought to be a log somewhere. Ah! What's this?'

He dragged the heavy table on one side and from underneath where it had been rescued a heavy, dusty volume bound in black leather, its pages beginning to yellow at the edges. With some effort he balanced it on his knee and turned crackling pages.

'Log all right!' Douglas exclaimed eagerly, peering with Vera over his shoulders. 'What does it say?'

'Give me time, man!'

Brooks flipped the pages. Up to January 21st 1929 the entries were quite normal. The ship had obviously been carrying a crew of fifty naval cadets. On

January 21st came the most surprising and significant entry of all:

* * *

January 21 — Cannot understand how we have gone off course during the night. The stars are different and the compass refuses to behave itself. In fact all the electrical apparatus is behaving erratically.

January 22 — We have drifted on to a strange ocean. It is quite uncharted. Horizon vastly extended. Sun and stars shine together. No sign of land.

January 23 — The men have mutinied! Supplies cannot last forever. There seems to be no explanation —

* * *

The entries stopped abruptly with a streak of the pen. Brooks closed the book slowly, then stood up with it under his arm.

'Somehow this ship passed into the fourth dimension while sailing, without the benefit of apparatus at that,' he said.

82

'From that premise we may assume that many other lost ships have probably done likewise. Planes too have usually vanished when over great bodies of water. Of course, we know that the vibratory rate is responsible for the transition from plane to plane, and we know too that water is a perfect conductor of all things electrical. I'm not sure of my ground here, but is it not possible — in the fashion that lightning strikes as a rule where it can find water? By the same token, perhaps over great oceans which must definitely attract the myriad and one vibrations and currents always streaming down through the atmosphere, there may exist at times an area, movable maybe, wherein the vibratory rate is different?

'A small thing like a ship might therefore float into one of these pockets — as might an airplane — and never get back, the current being powerful enough to shift the atomic makeup from one rate of vibration to another for all time?

'Yes, I think it is the only possible theory. Oceans at best are mysterious, full of the unexplained. Strange lights are

83

seen in them, St. Elmo's fire plays on the masts, weird electrical upheavals are common.'

Brooks sighed and stuck the book more firmly under his arm.

'Right or wrong, it's the only theory I can find. We're taking this book back home with us as proof. Now we'd better get outside again.'

6

The Voice

Returning to the broken companionway they fought their way up to the deck again. It was just as they reached it that night descended with the suddenness of a fused lamp.

'Hang it!' Brooks exclaimed from the dark. 'Can't be a scrap of refraction in this blasted plane. The light wave quirks are too thorough for my liking. You okay, Vera?'

'Okay,' she assented, rather dryly. 'I had the chance to practice being in the dark recently, remember. It's night in New York too,' she added. 'I can see the city lights.'

'Wish I could,' Douglas sighed wistfully. 'Be a comfort in this forsaken land.'

They found their way along the deck and so back to the beach again. Here

Douglas' voice floated out of the void in sudden alarm.

'Say, it's night! Do you realize that? We started on this trip at ten in the morning and we've hardly done anything yet. Now it's dark. That means that at least seven or eight hours have passed. I thought our vibratory visit was set for only two or three hours, Mason?'

'It was,' the physicist answered, with a trace of uneasiness. 'But then, how is one to judge? Time, space, our very bodies are different. For instance, if seven hours or so have gone by we ought to be hungry and thirsty but we're not. At least I'm not. How about you two?'

Douglas and Vera were surprised to find that they were not hungry either, and said so.

'Consumption of energy — bodily energy — must be different while we work at a new ratio, and therefore doesn't need replenishing as fast,' Brooks mused.

'You have an answer in science for everything, haven't you?' Vera asked irritably. 'Personally, this place is beginning to scare me. I feel we are so horribly, completely alone. I can at least see into our own world but it is only a shadowy plane, which I can't touch. I feel utterly cut off. For you two it must be even worse because you can only see this awful landscape. Mace, are you sure we'll get back?' she asked anxiously.

'Yes. Yes, of course,' he retorted. 'Mathematics prove it.'

'Mathematics! Last time you dabbled in math you forgot something. Remember? That machine?'

'For heaven's sake stop worrying me,' he growled. 'We'll be all right. Come on, let's walk. Standing here in this silence with that old ship near to us is tearing my nerves to rags.'

He turned and began to move. Douglas and the girl kept pace with him. They didn't talk any further. They felt too overwhelmed. They heard only the sound of those wavelets on the shore and the noise of their own feet crunching in sand. Not a vestige of a breeze, not the vaguest hint of life was brought to them. The aching, endless quiet and nothing more.

Then, with a rather surprising suddenness, their way was lighted by the full moon. It came over the incredibly distant horizon so rapidly they could see it moving. It looked utterly unlike the moon to which they were accustomed, for it bulged like a mammoth silver egg.

'For some reason or other this plane gives you stereoscopic vision when you look at the sky,' Brooks murmured, staring up. 'Light waves again, I guess. But at least things up there are more or less normal. The moon is in her right place and in her right phase. Stars are differently placed, though, and — *hmm*, that's odd!'

He broke off and stared wonderingly.

'What?' Douglas questioned.

For several minutes Brooks peered at the sky, before speaking again.

'That planet is Mars, and that one is Venus — low down there. But they look different. For one thing Mars has no red glimmer, and Venus has lost a good deal of her high albedo.'

'Albedo?' Vera repeated.

'Light reflecting quality!' Brooks showed

impatience at her ignorance. 'Now just why should they look different?'

'Maybe they're not the right planets,' Douglas suggested.

The physicist meditated for a moment or two, and then he caught hold of his sister's arm.

'Vera, how does the sky look to you?'

'Normal, praise be,' she answered. 'Though there are some new stars I can't account for, peculiar to this plane maybe. But the rest of the sky looks normal. Still it was the same way when I looked at it from New York.'

Brooks smiled with gratification.

'Which shows the sky is identical in both places!' he declared in satisfaction. 'Good! Then we have got Venus and Mars there, and they are different!'

'I'm more interested in returning home,' Vera sighed. 'The time keeps going on and we show no signs of getting back.'

'We will!' Brooks seemed quite unconcerned. 'Think of the amazing things we're discovering and try to use your brains a little.'

The girl said nothing as they continued

walking. Obviously his intense scientific interest in everything had blunted all his humane feelings.

It was perhaps half an hour later, as near as they could tell with time and distance so inexplicable, when they found themselves in the regions of the ruined city. It stood a pale and crumbled monument to vanished endeavor.

'Plenty of buildings still standing,' Brooks commented, glancing around in the pallid moonlight. 'Roofs are gone and the walls look sick, but we can perhaps take a quick survey.'

'We ought to feel sleepy,' Vera said, oddly. 'But we don't.'

'And until we do we'll keep going,' Brooks decided. 'Let's see what we've got in here.'

He led the way across crumbled stonework to the nearest half-demolished edifice and pushed on the massive metal door. Under the pressure it collapsed almost immediately, not because the lock had perished, but because the supporting stonework fell to the ground.

Beyond was a vision — an amazing

vision, lighted by the moon shining through the clear space where the roof had once been. There was the shell of an immensely long building, the walls towering up to perhaps a hundred feet, the metal shields still in place across the open spaces where windows had been. It was only by degrees that the trio realized that there were machines here, covered in the dust and chippings from the fallen roof.

'This the machine hall you saw from our plane, Vera?' Brooks inquired, surveying it.

'No. In any case it can't be. I couldn't see through walls, remember. The place I saw was a total ruin. This is another one entirely.'

'Interesting, too, unless I miss my guess,' the physicist muttered.

He stepped across to the nearest machinery and stood looking at it. Finally he knocked the dust from it with his haversack and looked more closely.

'Some kind of power generator, near as I can tell,' he commented finally. 'Light isn't too good. You two take a look around

91

and see what you can find.'

They went off together and thereupon Brooks proceeded to forget all about them. His scientist's soul was lost in the contemplation of these gigantic scientific engineering wonders wrought by a race of people now utterly vanished.

Brooks found all kinds of conjectures passing through his mind as he went from machine to machine and pondered upon their diversity and complexity. Who had done all this? Four-dimensional beings? Were they perhaps present and yet invisible? Somehow, though, this theory did not seem to fit.

By degrees, as Douglas and the girl explored the further regions of the hall, Brooks kept discovering huge dynamos of queer outline, transformers, great banks of resistances, all manner of electrical equipment of a high order, together with many things he did not understand at all.

Gradually it became clear to him that every one of them was so designed as to face a truly enormous creation like a tower rearing up to the sky from the very center of the hall. At the top of it, glinting in the moonlight, there appeared to be a massive sphere.

He frowned, an astonishing thought crossing his mind. There seemed to be no connection from one machine to another, yet each machine faced this tower. Surely not by coincidence? Perhaps transmission of power through radiation? Akin to radio? It was the dream of engineers in his own plane. Here, maybe, it had been accomplished. But the idea demanded a huge step from conjecture to proof. He'd need the daylight to make sure, anyway.

He was studying the tower pensively when he turned and looked round for his sister and Douglas, intent on getting their opinions. To his surprise they had vanished, but almost immediately he saw where. A door was leading into another hall beyond this one.

Turning, he strode towards it, entered yet another roofless building and beheld massive long disused telescopic equipment soaring towards the skeleton of a dome which had once been covered. He had hardly time to take in the fact that he was in a kind of observatory before an incredible feeling stole over him. At the same moment Douglas and Vera, quite nearby, must have felt it too for they half turned in alarm, then stood motionless.

It was an intense feeling of constriction, of being forced into involuntary paralysis. For a moment Brooks suspected that they were about to be returned to their own plane and hugged the *Kobenhavn* log the tighter to him in readiness. Then he realized that the sensation had no kinship to that overdue metamorphosis. Instead it was an iron rigidity that settled. Neither he, Douglas, nor Vera could budge an inch.

Then, as they waited tensely, they heard something. It was like a voice, and yet it was not a voice. It made no actual sound in the deserted spaces. Instead it crept into the senses and made itself understood as super-telepathy.

'You have crossed the electric eyes, my friends, and now you are to experience the unforgettable! Your ability to be here in this plane makes you worthy of it. Prepare yourselves for an explanation.'

Every word, every thought impulse

— since that was what it really was — was utterly distinct. Vaguely, Brooks understood. He, or his sister and Douglas, had crossed an invisible radiation somehow generated even after all else had stopped. It had set hidden scientific powers working. Telepathy. The absolute grip of mind and muscle. No matter how much they might have wished otherwise they were compelled to obey the science of a race long gone.

Slowly a sense of being lifted out of themselves stole upon them. They were compelled not only to see events, but to feel that they were a part of them. And yet, paradoxically, they were distinct and separated from the actual moment by untold ages.

7

Vision of the Past

Gradually things grew dark — even for Vera with her double vision. She would have cried out in terror only her muscles refused to work. Brooks, the most scientific, surmised what was happening, that their brains were being deliberately blacked out to everything except the impressions that were shortly to reach them.

For a while there was nothing. He was standing, like Douglas and Vera, utterly motionless staring into a void. There was no sound either. Even the four dimensional plane itself had not seemed so utterly quiet as this. It was death in life.

Then again that Voice which spoke in pure thought, which was clearly understandable.

'You cannot attempt to understand what you have seen around you. Not yet.

But if you ever do you will have earned the right to possess the heritage we have left you. What you are about to experience is purely a record of events left in readiness for the day when you outcast people of the Third plane would find your way back to your real heritage.

'We realize that in the very act of finding your way back you have proved yourselves scientific enough to understand at least some of the mighty heritage which is yours. I am not a man, not even a Voice, but a mentally recorded series of thoughts transmitted by a machine, the deep complexities of which you may one day understand. Now, by sensory perception you shall have an explanation.'

Suddenly the darkness was relieved and the paralyzed three gazed in wonder on a scene in which they seemed to be involved. They were looking into a gigantic hall of stone, its arched roof supported by pillars, its windows wide and giving onto a view of the eternal landscape so peculiar to this plane.

It was brilliantly lighted by both sunshine outside and concealed lighting inside. The three were apparently at the rear of the hall, looking over the heads of a multitude of seated people. They were people just like themselves, except for one thing. They had queerly fashioned eyes. Instead of a pupil and iris there was an organ made up of four facets!

The people consisted of both men and women, serious-faced, all of them strangely attired in the briefest of costumes and looking towards the far end of the mighty hall where four men and women — again with faceted eyes — were seated on a raised dais looking down on a separate crowd of people numbering maybe a thousand.

It was a fantastic vision indeed and so utterly real that it was hard to credit that it was only an incredibly accurate sensory impression of an event in long forgotten Time.

Thoughts that sounded like voices floated across the huge expanse.

'You men and women, led by Agra Libaflis, have been found guilty of the charges brought against you. The chief charge is that of subversive activity against the State nd Conclave of Scientists. One thousand of you have been found guilty, and by the law each and every one of you must suffer the same fate as your leader, Agra Libaflis.'

There was an unearthly silence for a while.

'Long ago such activity was punishable by death,' the message went on. 'But science decided that such a law was barbaric and served no useful purpose. It fails to train the criminal mind to right itself. In its place banishment was substituted, usually to some far part of our world. We, too, have decided on banishment for you, but one of such utter completeness that you can never return, no matter how much you may wish to do so. For the crime of trying to overthrow Science no punishment can be too stern.

'We the Supreme Judges of the Scientists, have decided that the entire thousand of you shall be banished to the Third Plane. We know that it exists as a material segment of our infinitely vaster world, a kind of Desert Island of matter. In the Third Plane you will be shorn of all the powers you possess here. Freedom of movement will be limited. You will find your world very small indeed.

'When you enter it, it will be without human life. From what you know of science you can try and build anew, start a fresh race indeed, if you wish, since there are women among you, some of you already mated.

'But to be sure that you can never return here, your eyes will be stripped of their outer lenses, that wonderful work of Nature which enables us to see in four dimensions! You will, as it were, become four-dimensionally blind, able only to see in three dimensions. Amongst the women of you, further operations will be made to ensure that whatever children there may be will, likewise, possess no trace of the eyes you have here. That is all!'

The scene faded, to be presently replaced by another view of a long operating theater. Since the surgeons and tables, with the victims thereon, seemed to recede to infinity, it seemed as if the entire condemned thousand were present here, undergoing the eye and — in the case of the females — the internal operations of which the Judge had spoken. It was a vision that lasted only briefly, to be replaced by a scene in a titanic hall of machines.

Here again the thousand were present, within the area of a huge magnetic instrument. Brooks, staring at it, realized it was a gigantic edition of the very machine he himself had made from Vera's description. Perhaps it was the identical machine itself.

Douglas, for his part, was not so interested in the machinery as in the eyes of the banished ones. He studied them as closely as he could. Then, slowly, the great crowd of people began to melt and finally disappeared. The laboratory was empty.

Very gradually blackness returned, and with it the Voice.

'You have witnessed what happened, my friend — how the remote ancestors of your Three-Dimensional Plane came into being. But for their transgressions there would never have been a populated Three-Dimensional Plane.

'You know that there is since you have

come from it. By rights your heritage is this world of four dimensions, which you can never fully appreciate until your eyes achieve again the four-dimensional power they should rightly possess.

'We surmised that, as time went on, humbled remote descendants of the Banished might find their way back here. For that reason we decided to leave them these machines and the chance to begin again. Master these machines, behave as true scientists, and you can begin again.

'We, by the very law of evolution, have advanced so far up the scale that we no longer need machines and so shall depart this planet. You have seen, my friends. Now you must reason — deeply!'

The Voice stopped and the awful blackness gradually became tinged with gray. Slowly, like a veil lifting, the obscurity gave way to the ruined observatory again with its cold moonlight. All trace or sign of the vision of the past had gone.

By degrees the paralysis abated, and finally ceased.

Brooks moved stiffly, clutched his

logbook again. He went over to where his sister and Douglas were rubbing their aching limbs painfully.

'Did that really happen?' the girl whispered. 'Or was it just a dream?'

'No, it happened. We have to realize that we are dealing with stupendous scientific power in this place. So much was explained in those few brief scenes, practically the whole history of the human race in fact. Or didn't you comprehend that?'

'I understand one thing,' Douglas said. 'In regard to that eye operation, I mean. The normal four-dimensional eye is made up of four facets, whereas ours is only a single lens. After the Thousand had been operated upon, their eyes looked like ours. Only they had a large fleshy piece left in the nasal corner where the four-dimensional surface lens had been cut away.

'According to the science of optics, that fleshy bit — which every human being has today in the nasal corner of the eye, but which of course has shrunk a good deal in the course of time — belongs to a time when we were saurians and had to have an extra membrane for underwater work. Most biologists believe that.

'It's called the *plica semi-lunaris*, by the way, and sometimes 'the third eyelid.' What I know now is that it never had anything to do with a saurian ancestry but with a four-dimensional one. The missing section must have been present in the children of the Banished, and so on down through the ages to today.'

'Good!' Brooks complimented him. 'Very good. That part of the revelation being optical you would of course grasp fully — but did you understand anything else?'

'Not clearly,' Douglas confessed, and Vera beside him shook her head in the moonlight.

'To me, it explains everything in our history that needs explaining,' the physicist said. 'It shows that there is no real connection between man and ape. The two are distinct breeds. Human beings were placed in our plane from here, when apes were no doubt the normal form of life, the kind of life that should inhabit the cramped confines of three dimensions. That is why the Missing Link has never been found. It explains too the marvelous science of the early races.'

For a second or two Brooks paused to allow his listeners to absorb these facts. 'Fresh from the wondrous science of this plane the original Thousand would build mighty cities and use wonderful science, but by degrees — with each fresh stage of evolution — knowledge, cut off from the source and their four-dimensional outlook destroyed, which would be bound to affect them adversely, physically and mentally — would begin to fade until at last the people became almost debased. Then, slowly, they began the upward swing again and so evolved to the present day with the real history lost in the mists of antiquity, or at the most mere garbled legend.

'Now we know why there are cities of surpassing wonder in the Sahara regions, why El Dorado must really have existed, why there must actually have been an Atlantis, withal overwhelmed by a catastrophe. They were the cities of the Thousand, and we are their successors, not ever yet clever enough to approach the genius they must have possessed.'

'Then we didn't spring from amoeba?' Douglas asked.

'No. Not in the Third Plane anyway. The ape probably sprang from that. Amoeba, fish, saurian, dinosaurs, ape. *Homo sapiens* is a distinct but mighty breed.'

There was an obvious pride in Brooks' voice as he claimed his connection with mankind, which sounded rather odd in the windless silences of the observatory. Douglas glanced at the girl as the physicist spoke again.

'Do you comprehend what we have here?' he breathed. 'All around us? In these machines there is power such as man never dreamed of in our little circumscribed three-dimensioned world!'

'But you don't understand any of it,' Vera pointed out, sensing the ambition in his voice.

'I could — given time.'

'That Voice, or whatever it was, said that this is our rightful heritage,' Douglas mused. 'In that case everybody in the world ought to share it. It is theirs — not ours. We could make a grand thing of humanity's future if this plane could be resurrected. In time I might even find out how to make eyes that are four-dimensional and thereby we could enjoy our full legacy.'

'Yes, that's true.' It was plain deep thoughts were going through the physicist's brain, thoughts other than those which prompted his next question. 'I just wonder where these four-dimensional people went? And why?'

'We may find out in time,' Douglas answered. 'We — '

Whatever he was going to say was lost, for all of a sudden the three of them felt a vicious tingling sweeping through their bodies. So swiftly did it come that they had hardly time to realize what had occurred, they found the ruined observatory fading from before their eyes.

Darkness. A flash of light that seemed to sweep from infinity.

All three of them fell heavily.

Dazed, they looked about them. They were lying on their backs on a deserted sidewalk, a street lamp casting a soft glow over their heads. Silently a car slid past towards the city center.

'We're back!' Vera cried hoarsely, getting up. 'Oh, thank heavens for that! We're back in the city!'

'Can you see Beyond?' Brooks demanded, catching her arm.

'Yes. It's the same as usual. But it's dark, of course. What do I care anyway?' Vera shrugged. 'We're back in our own plane, among our own people.'

'Confound it!' Brooks exploded abruptly. 'That logbook. It's gone!'

He searched round for it desperately, and Douglas and Vera helped him. Then he finally gave a sardonic chuckle.

'Never mind. I should have known. It isn't adapted to the vibration of this plane, so it just couldn't come any more than tomorrow can be a part of yesterday. My word will have to suffice.'

'There's a police officer down the road there,' Douglas murmured. 'With these provision packs on our backs and at this hour of night, we might be run in. Let's get moving.'

They went, as fast as they could. When finally they gained a recognizable street intersection they discovered they had only moved about three miles from their first starting point.

'You'd better stay the night at our place, Doug,' Brooks decided. 'We'll get a meal and a sleep, then we've the devil of a lot to talk over.'

8

Doubt

It was only when they got to bed that the three experienced the full weight of their weariness. Oddly enough, the moment they came back into their own time and space normal bodily conditions reasserted themselves and they felt indeed as if they had been wandering for ages without food or drink. As to the Time-discrepancy between planes, Brooks frankly had no explanation to offer since it involved deep mathematical issues.

It was ten the following morning before the manservant awakened each of them in turn. Immediately after breakfast, Brooks convened a council of action in the library.

'What we have discovered,' he said earnestly, tapping his fingers emphatically on top of the polished desk, 'opens a huge field of possibility — so huge one can't grasp it all at once. Unlimited power and prospects. That is what we have in the fourth dimension, and that is what we have to hold. Just discovering such wonders is of no use by itself. We have got to make a profit out of it.'

'Depends on what you call a profit,' Douglas said, studying Brooks' eager features. 'For my part, my views last night are the same as now. I believe we should try and give the people of the world the heritage to which they are rightly entitled.'

'And so do I,' Vera said promptly.

'You, Sis, are too inexperienced in the ways of science and the world to know anything about it,' the physicist said calmly. 'And you're not showing much vision either, Doug! One can't just give a thing as mighty as this to all the varied people of Earth. They'd abuse it. That is, without a leader,' he finished slowly.

Douglas gave him a sharp look. 'I may be wrong, Mason, but it sounds to me as though you want to turn the science we've discovered to your own personal advantage.'

'Right!' Brooks grinned sardonically. 'And why not? What does the ordinary man or woman know of science? They are born to be controlled, not to be controllers. I have a plan — a good one, too! Listen.'

He leaned forward across the desk intently.

'I am the master of this situation because I have the key to the unknown. I have the machinery that can get us there — and I have a sister who knows what is going on in both planes. On top of that I am the Chief Scientist of this city and that means one thing above all others — that I know as much, and more, of science than all the rest of the City Scientists put together.

'Now, I can't hope to master all those machines in the other plane off my own bat, for it would take too long. But I can take with me the best scientists the City Scientists possess and get them to help me.

'I can pool their knowledge and make myself acquainted with everything they discover. They will find things out individually and so each will supply an unrelated section of information, which I shall piece into the complete jigsaw. By that means I can become the supreme thinker while they simply have only sections of knowledge. There! Isn't that a grand idea?'

'But what about everybody sharing in the benefits?' Douglas demanded.

'Nobody can share in any benefits until everything is under control, can they? That's logical. We've got to get organized first.'

Douglas stared thoughtfully at the desk, and Vera rubbed her round chin as she cogitated. The physicist watched them for a moment or two. Then he got to his feet impatiently.

'If only either of you had the merest atom of science in your makeup you'd move a blamed sight quicker!' he snapped. 'My plan is the only one. With the knowledge I've got, I'm the obvious leader. We have the pearl of great price in our hands. The possibilities embrace revolutionary means of space travel, transmission of power by radio, thought-wave transference. We know those things already exist over there. There must be other wonders.'

Douglas raised his eyes from the desk last and looked to where the physicist was waiting grimly.

'Maybe you've worked it out okay,' he said. 'I don't like the ambitious flavor about it, but maybe that is because I am conservative.'

'In my view, Mace, you've got a bad attack of ambition,' Vera said, as her brother glanced at her. 'I can't do anything about it now. But if you get a good swift punch on the nose later, don't blame me!'

Brooks grinned. 'I can look after myself.' He glanced at his watch. 'Better get dressed to go out, both of you, we're due to give the City Scientists the surprise of their lives this morning. They'll find I'm turning my vacation to good account.'

Mason Brooks' eyes were glittering with a hard light as he turned away.

Because he was Chief Physicist, Mason Brooks had no difficulty in calling together the six authorities who directed

114

the destinies of the City Scientists. But, though his position was the highest in the research field, he did not possess the power of the last word.

This power lay with the six themselves, and ultimately with Walbrook Dean, the sixty-three-year-old multimillionaire physicist, whose money and brains, under Congressional authority, had banded the City Scientists together.

This gray-haired, imperturbable man with the shrewd brown eyes sat at the head of the long table when at an hour before noon Brooks had at last succeeded in assembling everybody.

As usual Brooks did not waste any time. Standing up he surveyed the faces, particularly those of his sister and Douglas is they sat in rather dubious silence.

'Gentlemen, do you admit the existence of the fourth dimension?' Brooks asked at length.

There was a surprised silence, then Bainbridge the mathematician nodded.

'Theoretically, yes.'

'That theory, gentlemen, is now a fact!

I have found the fourth dimension, and explored it, in company with my sister here and Dr. Ashfield.'

Not by the merest flicker of an eyelid did Walbrook Dean reveal that he was surprised. He looked at his colleagues and read expressions varying between downright incredulity and polite wonder.

'Perhaps you would explain in detail?' asked Jones, a geologist.

'Willingly!'

And Brooks did, adding neither more nor less than had actually occurred.

'I know it is hard to believe,' he concluded, 'I could have brought back proof with me in the shape of the logbook of the *Kobenhavn*, but the vibratory differences between this plane and that prevented me.

'You will have to take my word for it that such a plane, and such a log book, really exists. In that log book is the signed statement of a trusted master mariner to the effect that he was lost in a strange land.'

'Assuming that you have found this fourth dimension, Mr. Brooks, what do

116

you wish of us?' Walbrook Dean asked. 'Surely you had some reason for summoning us other than just to hear your story?'

'Of course.' Brooks nodded his sleek head. 'I want you to ask Congress for a financial grant, so that some hundreds of 'transition' machines may be manufactured, by which the best scientists in the world may be transported into this other dimension to study its intricacies.

'The machine I have, copied from one in the fourth dimension, is only capable at full capacity of dealing with three people. Then it exhausts itself. So of course many machines would be needed.'

Brooks waited in ill-disguised impatience while the dean pondered. Then Walbrook Dean's eyes strayed to Vera, and finally back to the physicist again.

'According to your story, Mr. Brooks, your sister was blinded, given artificial eyes, and then found she could see into the fourth dimension. The facts about the eye operation have leaked into the press, of course, and I understand that you, Dr. Ashfield, were removed from the register because of your activities?'

'True,' Douglas nodded. 'But I don't quite see what it has to do with the case. We have seen the fourth dimension.'

'As to that, I am in no position to agree or disagree. But obviously I cannot inform Congress that the dimension was discovered because an eye surgeon operated on Miss Brooks contrary to the wishes of the Ophthalmic Council. That would put things in a bad light right at the start.

'In the second place, Mr. Brooks, it is common knowledge by now that your experiments in matter-into-matter were the root cause of your sister losing her sight. You caused an appalling and costly explosion. Do you think, with this in mind, with no other proof at all but your own word and a story about a logbook of a vanished ship, that Congress would be willing to grant huge sums of money in the creation of machinery designed by you?

'Do you further think that any scientist would trust his life to your apparatus, having in mind the tragic consequences of your other experiment?'

Color crept into Brooks' face and neck. 'But I've already done it!' he shouted indignantly. 'If we went and came back, so can anybody else!'

'We have only your word that you have done it, Mr. Brooks. Congress would require more proof than that. Nor would the mere fact that your sister claims she can see into the fourth dimension suffice. As I understand it she gave out the news that she was still half blind, even after the operation.'

'I told her to do that, for security reasons.'

'A pity. It rather spoils your own case. Tell me, Dr. Ashfield, as an oculist, can you see anything different about Miss Brooks' eyes? Anything that might imply she can seen another plane?'

'Well, no,' Douglas admitted grudgingly. 'I don't know even now how it happened. It just — did.'

'Which would not suit Congress,' Walbrook Dean sighed.

'Gentlemen, I regard this as an insult to my knowledge and position,' Brooks said, keeping his temper with difficulty.

Dean leaned forward, his arms on the shining table.

'Do you want frankness?' he asked quietly.

'Certainly! It can't be worse than insults, anyway.'

'Very well. It is a well-known fact that you are a clever man, and an ambitious one. Time and again you have tried to advance your position by inventing the most astonishing scientific devices — the matter-into-matter machine was one of them. Up to now you have made no definite progress because we of the City Scientists have to keep a tight rein over science's progress, if only for the public good.

'This effort of yours might quite easily be — forgive me — another stunt! We certainly would get into trouble with Congress if we tried to get financial backing. I suggest that you provide absolute proof. Perhaps you can get that logbook here or else make us see into the fourth dimension as Miss Brooks does. Then, and only then, we'll go further.'

For a long time Brooks stared at the impersonal face fixedly.

'Bluntly, you dismiss the whole idea?' he snapped.

'Yes — for your good and ours. If it were a lesser scientist, we would have reported the whole thing as a clever trick to get money for scientific experiments but, being you, I am open to conviction.'

Brooks kicked his chair aside.

'Serves me right for wasting my time,' he said, his face white with anger. 'Thank you, gentlemen. And I'll not forget you for it, either!'

He jerked his head to his sister and Douglas and they followed him out into the paneled corridor. He closed the Board Room door with a vicious slam.

'Now you know how it feels,' Douglas murmured, as they made their way towards the exit.

'What do you mean by that?' the physicist rasped.

'I was hauled up before the Ophthalmic Council and afterwards kicked out on my ear, thanks to you. Now you've got the same thing. Not kicked out, maybe, but you're not believed.'

'I should care,' Brooks answered. 'I'll solve those other-plane machines myself. I gave them their chance.'

'For your own ends,' Vera put in. 'You meant to use them. You said you did. I think Dean saw through your little plot.'

'Oh, shut up!' Brooks was too incensed to pursue the subject further, but, by the time they had reached Fifth Avenue, he was cool again — grimly cool.

He said nothing until after lunch. By that time he appeared to have made up his mind. Peremptorily he ordered Douglas and Vera into the laboratory.

'We're going back there,' he announced. 'Not for just a few weeks, but indefinitely. Once on the other side I think we can keep recharging ourselves. Since they have as good as called me a liar at the City Scientists I'm quitting. Your practice has gone anyway, Doug. We can spend the afternoon packing a few crates with provisions and other necessities.'

He fell to thinking for a moment.

'Perhaps it's better this way, come to

think of it,' he went on. 'If we can solve those machines ourselves, it means no sharing. I suppose, really, I could finance transition machines myself, but why the devil should I? That's Congress' privilege. Well, we're going. You two can come with me?'

His tone implied that he fully expected it.

'We'll come, if only to keep the brakes on your ambitions,' Vera answered. 'From my standpoint, as a woman, I can see an awful lot of trouble coming up, if you get your hands on unlimited scientific power.'

'You're a feminine little fool,' he answered briefly. 'And let's hear your grudge, Doug, while we're at it.'

'No grudge,' he answered. 'I'm distressed about the whole thing, really. I wanted people to know, to be able to use this wonderland we have found.'

'They will — later,' Brooks said, grandly. 'Well, let's start packing up. Fetch that crate over here, Sis. I'll check the apparatus and make sure everything's okay.'

9

Riddle of the Planets

It was shortly before seven o'clock in the evening when they made their second leap into the other plane. With them, likewise altered in vibratory rate, went three packing cases full of needful things. The experience of the transition was not quite so unnerving this time. As before they found themselves lying on their backs on the hard ground with the grotesque moon and icily shining stars above them. Again that landscape which swept to eternity stretched away in every direction.

'Good!' Brooks murmured, getting up. 'The cases have come too. I rather thought they would. Difficult to decide just how much alteration in atomic setup they needed.'

The girl and Douglas stood up beside him as he looked towards the distant ruins of the city.

'Going to hunt for that logbook?' Vera enquired.

'No. If they can't take my word they can go to blazes. We'll camp in the machine hall. Give me a hand with the crates.'

So work commenced, and work it certainly was. The cases were all heavy, but at least the apparent distances were foreshortened by the odd light-values of the plane. In all, with Vera helping, it took them about an hour of normal time to transport their belongings to the first machine hall. Then Brooks switched on three portable floodlights he had brought along in Crate Number One.

Unpacking began, working in an area that seemed curiously bright even for the floodlights. It occurred to Douglas after a while what was wrong. Suddenly, staring behind him, he caught the physicist's arm.

'Say, look!' he breathed. 'The light's right behind us, but there are no shadows.'

Somehow it was eerie. All three of them deliberately interposed their bodies

125

between the light and the nearest wall, but the light shone on steadily, unmasked.

'That is what has been worrying me all along,' Vera decided at length. 'I knew there was something odd — peculiar.'

'A shadow is two dimensional in that it has only length and breadth,' Brooks said pensively. 'We know that light waves not only don't go straight in this plane, as they're supposed to, but that they move with infinite velocity. A shadow is the direct outcome of three dimensions, not four. That, and the light wave differences, probably explains their absence.'

Satisfied, at least in his own mind, he turned back to emptying the crates. Gradually provisions, small machine tools, bedding, electrical instruments, clothes — all kinds of things were carefully unloaded, including portable cooking apparatus fitted with its own batteries.

It took them another two hours to finish their task and get the bedding arranged. Then in the double light of ghostly moon and floodlamps they squatted down to a meal before the cone of heated element standing in the center of the vast hall.

'If stored energy were not an everyday thing to us, we'd be mighty cold,' Brooks reflected, eating a sandwich.

'And dark,' Douglas added. 'Except for the moon.'

Suddenly, in spite of herself, Vera gave a little shiver.

'This place still frightens me,' she said, as the two men looked at her. 'Whether it is because I can see two worlds at once, or whether there is really something deadly about it, I don't know. But — well — I'm still scared!'

'Nerves,' Brooks decided calmly.

'I'm not so sure. I have the feeling that I am being watched all the time by somebody I can't see. I've noticed it ever since we first came here on that other trip.'

Her brother's keen eyes traveled in a wide circuit as he surveyed the hall.

'The place is stone dead,' he proclaimed finally. 'Just try curbing your imagination. I certainly don't feel it. Do you, Doug?'

'No. But this place is a creepy spot all the same.'

'Perhaps, being a woman, I'm more sensitive,' Vera mused. 'And yet, after all, we didn't solve where the people who owned this city went to, did we? They might be all around us, invisible, watching.'

Her brother stopped with a sandwich halfway to his mouth.

'They might have — evolved,' he said. 'The Voice did say that they had done that, but it also said that they had departed from this planet. Anyhow, why the devil should they stop here when they can roam the universe?'

'It's a problem we'll have to solve finally,' Douglas said thinking. 'At least we must try and find out where they went. As for Vera's fears, I don't think we ought to deride any emotion here. It might provide a clue.'

Brooks grinned. 'You're in love with Vera. To me she is just a sister — and a pretty crazy one at that. Best thing we can do is finish this meal, then get some sleep. When daylight comes, we'll get busy in real earnest.'

They slept without interruption, again

to awake again beneath that crazy, prominence-girdled sun creeping across the dull blue unclouded sky. Breakfast over, Brooks outlined his plans.

'We have this hall, and the next one — the observatory — to examine first,' he explained. 'As near as I can tell, most of the stuff in here is electrical and therefore right up my street. You, Doug, as an oculist and expert in lenses will probably find the observatory more to your taste. Find out everything you can and we'll compare notes when the sun reaches the meridian. That, as near as we can tell, should be noon.'

'And what do I do?' Vera asked dryly 'Twiddle my thumbs?'

'Either that or prepare the dinner.'

Her brother turned away actively, small electric testing instruments bulging in his pockets. The girl watched him hurry toward the distant regions of the hall.

'Dinner my foot!' she said calmly, turning to Douglas. 'I'm coming with you.'

He smiled and nodded. Together they left the huge main hall with its open roof and walked through to the next one. Now that they came to look at the observatory properly, they noticed that, apart from the giant central reflecting telescope there were perhaps two hundred other optical machines, but of what precise nature remained to be seen.

After the girl had wandered off to investigate on her own account, Douglas began to prowl round the apparatus. In a while he realized that he had walked into a wonderland. There were photo-micrometers of incredible delicacy, as perfect as the day they had been abandoned; television equipment which apparently did not need any transmitter at the other end to deliver its images. Rather it seemed only to need current for the generation, of a 'seeing-beam' of its own and retransmit the result back into the scanning screen.

Then there were lens-grinding machines, flawlessly cast. There were microscopes so powerful that a strand of hair looked like a thigh for thickness and bits of dust like crystalline rock. Other instruments were incomprehensible altogether and could only explain themselves when and if power was finally restored.

In her search Vera came across radio equipment, as distinct from the television. There was X-ray apparatus, and instruments with ground glass lenses, which perhaps emitted rays of different frequencies, known and unknown.

She saw cameras, color screens, spectro-heliographs, thermoscopes, electroscopes, curiously distorting mirrors that gave the impression of looking into several dimensions at once. She wandered amidst them, and marveled. But she could not hope to understand them.

Finally she rejoined Douglas again beside the giant reflector and they compared results.

'That our vanished friends were masters of Science is quite evident,' Douglas commented pensively. 'How many of their devices work we shan't know unless Mason finds how to get the power going.'

'And this is only one hall,' Vera exclaimed. 'There are dozens of others. I know that. It sort of — of overwhelms you when you think of it!'

131

Douglas nodded slowly and then turned to look at the huge telescope. Its great central universal mountings were obviously powered by electric motors, dusty and silent So complicated was the telescope that it took him some time to find the tiny eyepieces amidst the adjustment screws. When at last he discovered them — as apart from the reflector mirrors which he simply did not understand at all — he glued his eyes to the lenses and saw dark blue sky.

To his surprise the monster instrument was so marvelously balanced it moved gently under the pressure of his hand. Evidently the motors were to keep it tracking when necessary for protracted observation. Gently he shifted the giant. At last he sucked in his breath in amazement.

Something round, apparently two feet in diameter, was clear as crystal before him. Surely it could not be a planet! Not at such a size. In his own plane he recalled that even the four-hundred-inch giant at Mount Everest only made a planet look no larger than a melon. This result was incredible.

Yet a planet it certainly was, unclouded and drenched in sunshine! He could descry green foliage, deep blue seas, cities of fantastic whiteness. As he looked and wondered, the cities melted into thin air and there was only sun-drenched landscape.

'What the devil!' he whispered, pressing his fingers to his eyes.

Vera looked at him quickly.

'Anything wrong?'

'I don't know. I think I'm going crazy.'

He looked up at the sky through the broken roof girders. There was only one planet that could be within range of the instrument in its present position.

'Venus!' he exclaimed. 'But she ought to be heavily clouded, but she isn't. There are several cities — or were until they faded.'

'Faded?' the girl repeated, mystified.

'Something interesting?' asked Brooks, lounging in with a preoccupied expression.

Douglas turned to him quickly.

'Take a look through here and tell me if

I'm seeing things.'

As it happened Douglas found it was not necessary for him to desert the eyepieces. The telescope had six sets in all, all tuned prismatically to a central receiving mirror which, when power was available to liven its energized mercury surface, cast its reflections on to the giant mirror in the circular pit underneath the instrument.

So three pairs of eyes stared into the monster, intently. Even for Vera the view was more or less normal since space was superimposed on space, and in her own plane the daylight rendered Venus invisible anyway.

Once again those cities merged into view, extensive, exquisitely designed, the last dream of a master-architect. Then, once more, they faded like mist. The three pairs of eyes searched the planet restlessly but no other city was visible. There were only deep blue oceans and powdery sun-drenched land.

'Venus all right,' Brooks confirmed, though his voice showed he was shocked at this disavowal of known scientific facts.

'How about Mars?'

The giant swung again and after some maneuvering settled on the smaller planet. It wasn't red, not even ocher-colored, and the desert appearance was entirely absent.

Instead it was definitely a world of cities, deep gray cities, much as Earth's might look from another world. There were oceans too, and fairly prosperous-looking landscapes if the cultivated fields under the weak sunshine were any guide.

Slowly Brooks withdrew his eyes from the lenses and stood for a while in deep thought. He turned at last to find his sister and Douglas looking at him expectantly.

'I said the first night we came here that Mars and Venus looked different,' he remarked. 'Now I know I was right. Mars has lost his red color and is no longer a dead world. Venus, on the other hand, has lost her cloud cover and therefore her reflective surface which gave her such a high albedo. But this is incredible!' he broke off. 'Why so different?'

He bit his underlip with vexation

because he could not find an immediate solution to the problem. Mysteries, especially when they disproved the scientific facts of ages, annoyed him.

'Of course, space looks as different in the fourth dimension as land does,' he mused.

'How do you explain those melting Venusian cities?' Douglas asked.

'I just don't. I'm a physicist, not a magician. All I can say is that Venus has a civilization far higher than that of Mars. The beauty of Venus' vanishing cities proves it. They were far ahead in design of anything Mars possesses.

'Mars, apparently, has a civilization about the same as ours — normal plane, I mean. As for our being able to see the planets so clearly, I imagine, unknowingly, that we are looking at them through a space curved and foreshortened by the fourth dimension, apart from the tremendous power of this instrument, of course.'

'But does the fourth dimension explain their utterly different appearance?' Douglas demanded.

'I presume it does. But don't ask me how.'

Brooks sighed and scowled over the problem. At last he gave a shrug.

'No use trying to solve what we don't know. We'll have to walk before we can run. I've been taking a look around that other hall, by the way, and I've found plenty.'

With something of an effort, Douglas and the girl withdrew their attention from the telescope and watched Brooks as he paced slowly up and down. In every move he betrayed an intense eagerness from the things he had discovered.

'More I see of the next hall the surer I become that our departed scientists had mastered the secret of power from the sun transmitted direct through the air,' he said.

'You've seen that central tower-like instrument with the ball at the top? Well, I climbed up to it.'

Brooks stopped his pacing, a gleam in his eyes.

'It's made of some kind of metal I never heard of. It is possible, of course, that certain metals, or combination of metals, can attract radiation unto themselves and absorb it, much in the same way as tourmaline crystals polarize light, though that of course is in a different order of science. What I mean is this:

'To judge from the wiring of this ball it absorbs power from the atmosphere, which can only mean the sun, and then transmits it from a specially designed antennae to all parts of the hall — in fact very probably to all parts of this city. I think each machine picks up the power that way. A big radius might be affected; I've yet to discover the extent of the transmission.'

'Sounds interesting,' Douglas admitted. 'How do you start to prove your theory?'

'I'm studying the layout of the switches,' Brooks answered. 'If their arrangement comes anywhere near anything I understand I am going to risk moving some of them and see what happens.' Pausing, he consulted his notebook. 'That's what I came to tell you. And I came here also to find out what you have discovered as well, of course.'

Briefly Douglas related his own findings and Vera added hers.

The physicist nodded.

'Good! In due time we'll find out just what makes everything tick. Well, I'm going back to that tower plant to study it.'

He went off with long strides and Douglas looked after him.

'Watertight mind,' he murmured. 'For my part I'm a darned sight more interested in finding out how the planets have changed their faces. Still, I suppose we can't do anything more about it now. Better see what else there is.'

10

Science Without End

When they had about exhausted the resources of the observatory, they went through the further doorway and so out into the great crumbled expanses of what had once probably been the City's heart, a heart that had been made up of huge buildings and massive terraces.

'Something occurs to me,' Douglas said thoughtfully, gazing round in the shadowless sunlight. 'This city, when it was in full life, could have looked very like those vanishing cities we saw on Venus. The stone is similar — whitish. Dust and age have dimmed it now, of course.'

Vera nodded.

'It is a thought,' she agreed, but she had to drop the subject because she simply had not the knowledge to carry it on.

They began to walk, slowly. Inevitably

they covered greater distances than they had intended due to their inability to determine length and extension. Ten minutes of advance across the crumbled ruins had put the two halls out of sight and they now faced another hall, or rather the remains of one with only a single wall standing. The girl surveyed it pensively.

'This is the one I saw from our own plane — from the park!' she exclaimed. 'I can see the park superimposed behind it. There! That's the electronic machine I described to Mace.'

In a few minutes they were in a long disused aisle with the silent giants of an abandoned science on both sides of them. Douglas looked at the electronic machine, but beyond noticing that it was similar, on a gigantic scale, to the one Brooks had constructed he understood but little about it. Nor were the other machines within his field of knowledge. Every one apparently was electrical, but the great majority resembled objects like searchlights. There were huge lenses and, behind them, two bars like the electrodes of a carbon arc.

'Wouldn't want searchlights here, surely?'

he asked the girl, puzzled. She raised and lowered her shoulders helplessly.

Further along the aisle they came upon an instrument like an organ. There were endless stops, pedals, switches, and plugs. Inside it, a maze of complicated wiring. Perched on top of it was a frame of ground glass about four feet square.

'Do you know something,' the girl said slowly, looking about her. 'This place looks like — like an arsenal. Those search-light things might be ray-projectors. We have similar instruments in our own army back home anyway. And this thing here might be a sort of television thing for watching troop movements. Just a guess, but you never know.'

Douglas nodded rather wonderingly. Then he looked attentively at the multiple master-switchboard. Most of the switches were connected up to the instruments by fine silvery wire, which was within a casing of hard insulation.

Douglas' fingers itched to try one, but he refrained for fear of letting loose forces beyond his control. Finally his gaze settled on a lever. It was firmly embedded in a slot in the metallic floor, but there was no trace of the object to which it was connected.

'Pull it!' the girl urged. 'Can't do any harm, surely?'

Douglas hesitated. After a moment of indecision, he seized the lever with both hands and pulled it towards him. Perhaps two hundred yards away a section of the metal floor, with debris on top of it, suddenly caved inward. There was the muffled rumble of sliding rock and earth plunging below.

'Underground!' Vera cried excitedly. 'We've found something!'

She turned and hurried towards the area with Douglas close behind her. When they pulled up short, they found themselves gazing down into a black emptiness about fifteen feet square with the dim evidence of a slanting metal floor leading up to the opening.

'Are you risking it?' the girl asked.

'Wait here,' Douglas ordered. He left her while he raced back across fantastic distances to the main hall next to the observatory for his torch. Brooks, in the further reaches studying the tower, glanced at him but nothing more.

In five minutes Douglas had rejoined the girl. Switching on the torch beam he played it on a sloping floor that went down — deep down — into the depths of the earth.

'Let's go,' he murmured, taking her arm.

As near as they could tell, they went downward for half a mile before the floor suddenly leveled out and expanded into a huge underground space, obviously machine-drilled. It extended far beyond the powerful beams of Douglas' torch on every side, and the light reflected back from metals and glasslike substances.

'By the level of New York we're not far short of a mile down,' the girl said. 'I've been taking note.'

Her voice echoed in the expanse. Carefully, half afraid, they went forward again to the nearest source of reflection. It proved to be a mighty affair like the cultivated product of a modern tank. It was streamlined, tractored, bristling with queer armament and fitted with a conning tower on which lay a residue of dust.

There was not just one tank, but hundreds, thousands, as far as ever the torch beam could reach. No doubt they were supplemented by other forms of armament beyond this again.

In another direction were orderly files of stacked robots, shoulder to shoulder, motionless, their lensed eyes and crystalline bodies reflecting the glare. For many minutes Douglas and the girl walked down the center aisle between them, gaining a rough idea of the myriads of them there must have been stored down here.

Then they came to objects like silver shuttles with vestigial wings sprouting from the sides.

'Aircraft, of sorts,' the girl murmured. 'Far ahead of anything we've got. This is an underground military dump, or something very like it.'

'Yes, yes, that's right.' Douglas' voice was serious, so much so that Vera turned to him in the torchlight.

'What's wrong Doug? It's a discovery, isn't it?'

'An unpleasant one,' he responded. 'Do I have to tell you that you have an ambitious brother, or do you know that already?'

Vera was silent for a while, then she gave a little sigh.

'I see what you mean. You think that if he saw all this stuff here he might try and use it as a means of conquest?' She drew a deep breath. 'But how could he? There's nothing to conquer. And he can't use these things in our own plane.'

'He might find a way. He discovered how to bring crates from There to Here, so he might find a method of getting stuff like this from Here to There. If that failed, populated Mars might take his fancy. I know this a big assumption, and maybe unfair to Mason, but he's the kind of man who believes in big things. He's pretty bitter about the way the City Scientists turned him down, remember.'

'Then we'll say nothing about this,' the girl decided. 'Let's get back before he starts looking for us.'

Retracing their steps, they reached the ruined hall again before any signs of

Mason Brooks became visible. Then, when he had closed the door trap again and covered it realistically with more debris, Douglas returned to the actuating lever and studied its base. Finally he turned it in his hands and it began to unscrew, eventually parting from the socket in the floor-slot.

Carefully he put a slab of stone over the slot, then looked at the girl as he weighed the lever in his hands.

'So long as we keep the lever and he has other things on his mind, he's unlikely to find anything,' he said. 'We can hide this — here.'

He climbed up the bulk of a nearby machine and placed the lever behind its topmost ledge. The chances of Brooks finding it, or even then guessing its purpose, were remote.

'As to the rest of this stuff, I don't know much about it,' Douglas decided, looking around. 'But I may later. We'd better see how Mason is progressing. He may have the key to the whole outfit in that central tower plant he's studying.'

* ★ ★

Mason Brooks certainly had the key, but to discover just how it worked was not a task overcome in a few minutes. For many days, and part of some nights, he worked on equations and notes.

He forced his keen scientific mind to the utmost to work out the details of the complicated sciences involved in the control of the central power-tower. He seemed no longer in doubt that this was just what it was.

A week passed, time in which all three had gradually become accustomed to their surroundings and had discovered practically everything the ruined city contained. Then a fortnight . . .

In three weeks Brooks announced that he had solved the problem. Over a breakfast prepared by the girl, following a night during which he had been scribbling by the light of a portable lamp, he made the results of his research known.

'That central tower contains a metal attractor at the apex,' he explained. 'It is a well known fact that the sun gives off a vast surplus of energy which we have never found a way to utilize. But not so these scientists. They devised a metal with an atomic setup able to absorb these radiations — seventy-five percent of them anyway. This metal, when it has absorbed them, changes its atomic makeup of its own accord, similar but much faster to uranium changing into lead. The resultant energy given off by the change, is transmitted to the power transformers in the base of the tower.

'Those towers, on the moving of certain switches, give power — atomic power — to the machines. They pick up the transmission as an aerial picks up radio waves, and thereby begin to function. The actual radiation in terms of normal energy is not much, but expressed in terms of atomic energy it is stupendous.

'In other words and put briefly, that ball arrangement can absorb enough atomic energy from the sun during its daily race through the sky, to keep this city going for two months. Repeated daily you can see what would happen. The area it covers seems to be infinite, like everything else that functions by wavelength in this cock-eyed place.'

'Then it has been absorbing energy for untold generations?' Vera questioned.

'Yes. But the energy has been passing off harmlessly through a separate earthing circuit, otherwise the whole apparatus would have consumed itself long ago. I tested what I thought was this earthing circuit and it smashed my voltmeter.

'Since it is a Fry and Merrins instrument and goes up to maximum readings it showed two things — colossal power, and the power in existence *now*! Since I have studied the switch layout, I know just how to shunt the power from the 'waste' circuit to the normal circuit. And that is just what I intend to do this morning.'

'Once that is done, you think that every machine ought to function by just handling the controls?' Douglas said.

'They should.'

His observations brought breakfast to an abrupt conclusion and then they all three headed into the center of the hall.

Obviously quite sure of himself now and studying his notes at intervals, Brooks went to work on the controls of the towers. Finally, after moving a series of switches, he pulled the heavy master-switch free of the top contacts and jammed it in the lower ones.

There was a sound — the first the three had ever heard in this plane outside of the noises they themselves had made. It was a deep, purring hum of power, power flawlessly smooth, flowing through apparatus made by master engineers.

'It works!' Brooks exulted, color in his pale cheeks. 'I was right. Look at those dynamos over there! They must have been on open switch ready to pick up transmission right away.'

In a far corner of the hall were six huge, flawlessly balanced generators, spinning to a rising surge of power, their central shafts revolving so true that they seemed to be motionless.

'They must be to power the instruments which do not rely on radiated power,' Brooks decided. 'The others, though, should use this tower's broadcast energy. Let's see — '

He hurried over to the nearest machine, a complicated device rather like a loom. The moment he pressed the switches, metallic arms began to move gently, gathering speed. Fascinated, the trio watched as by mechanical processes the machine drew out long lengths of synthetically made stuff like cotton and began to weave them crosswise into a tightly-knit fabric.

'Clothes, carpets, tapestries!' Brooks exclaimed. 'It's an incredibly efficient automatic loom.'

They had suddenly entered a scientist's paradise. Each machine responded to the movement of switches and picked up the disseminated power.

They found they had equipment that created tabloids by breaking down and rebuilding the very atoms of the atmosphere. Others were mobile and moved about as vacuums and excavators, shoveling away rubbish and masonry by magnetic means.

There were automatic trip-hammers, drills, welding instruments, pulverizers, surgical apparatus perfect beyond imagination

. . . And in the observatory the radio and television equipment were ready for the using. In fact the task was to decide what the astounding machinery could *not* do!

Finally, towards evening, the three were satiated with discovery. They sat before a huge powered radiator eating some of the delicious synthetic food and discussing their achievements.

'One could build this city anew,' Brooks said, thinking. 'We have everything necessary to do it. We can create metal and stone just as easily as we can destroy it. We have excavators, mobile cranes. What we have not got is the labor — and, oddly enough, there don't seem to be any robots which might help.'

Vera's eyes strayed to where Douglas was sitting and he smiled rather grimly as he thought of the thousands of them packed away in the underground.

'We might perhaps get labor here,' Brooks went on slowly. 'If we could once get people here, we could do a great deal.'

'That's been my idea from the start,' Douglas reminded him. 'Everybody ought to share in this. We could build a city in this place that would make any normal city an utter back number. But after what happened to us how are we going to do it?'

'Offhand I don't know,' Brooks continued. 'But I have a notion twisting in the back of my mind. Frankly, I have another problem absorbing me at the moment. Those changed planets. I haven't forgotten about them, you know. We know that at least Mars is inhabited and maybe Venus too, and we have the radio equipment working too. It utilizes ultra short waves. I'm wondering if we might try a radio communication.'

'Good idea,' Douglas agreed. 'Since we seem to have foreshortened space in this realm, a message might not be hindered as it is in our own plane.'

The idea decided upon they acted. When supper was over, they went into the great observatory, floodlighted now by the normal lamps still embedded in the cracking walls, Brooks settled himself before the radio equipment, satisfied that at last he was tackling something he really understood.

It took him perhaps ten minutes of fishing with the transmission controls before he was satisfied that a short-wave carrier was going forth, aimed as near as his mathematics could judge it, at Venus' position in the night sky. Mars had yet to appear over the horizon.

'Earth calling Venus,' he intoned into the microphone. 'If you hear me show some sign. Earth calling.'

For nearly twenty minutes he kept repeating his announcement, but no response came through the speakers.

Just as he was about to give up the task, something happened!

11

Ways and Means

Each of the three felt it simultaneously — an immense flowing of power about them, the conviction that somebody or something was present with them in the great roofless hall. Brooks turned very slowly and gazed at the astonished faces of his sister and Douglas. They were staring into emptiness, expecting to see something materialize any moment.

As yet, however, nothing untoward was visible. Nevertheless they knew, with every instinct they possessed, that intelligence was near them, intelligence so immense, so transcendental, that their human minds were cowed into submissive attention before it

'You cannot see me, my friends,' said a voice. If it was a voice. Like the thought-wave instrument they had encountered at first, it seemed they felt words instead of heard them.

'I — we — have known for some time of your arrival in this plane,' it went on. 'You need not waste time trying to get into touch with the second world. I was intending to come here in any case. I — we — represent the race from which you came. Our evolution has been such that our bodies no longer signify anything. Long ago our minds merged into one great thinking unit.

'Matter we do not need, or use. Even our cities, which you saw through the reflector, are only a figment of our thoughts. Before you could pry too closely into forbidden things, we willed our domain out of being. To your limited senses it vanished.

'On the other planet, which you call Mars, there exists matter of a lower order which, even so, is still generations ahead of yourselves, existing as it does in four instead of three dimensions. For that reason knowledge is greater and the physical body is more adapted to understanding the manifold problems at which you balk.

'From your own three-dimensional plane both planets appear deserted. Or at least one seems dead and the other wreathed in cloud. The cloud is merely a product to keep your greedy eyes from probing our secrets, and the dead aspect of Mars is due to the fact you see it three-dimensionally instead of in its true perspective.'

'Can we not see you?' Brooks demanded, staring into the air.

'How can one ever see a thought?' asked the Presence dryly. 'No, you cannot see me, nor do you hear me. You merely sense my — our — being here. We are interested in your activities, interested that you have reached so far upward on the journey to reclaiming your lost heritage.

'You are the children of the original Thousand Outcasts, of course. You have heard the story of your ancestors, and since I have read your own story from your minds, you need not explain anything. You propose to try and master this machinery.'

'That was my idea,' Brooks assented. 'Or maybe you will not permit that?'

'On the contrary, we — I — shall watch your activities with interest. If we feel you have qualified to be the possessors of greater knowledge, we shall give it, and help you to return to your full status. If, on the other hand, we decide that there is still too much of the beast in you to allow you to control great science, we shall remove everything from you. It is for you yourselves to decide what our decision shall be.'

'If I may speak, I feel that this heritage is not ours alone,' Douglas put in quickly. 'It belongs to the entire human race. They are as much descended from the Thousand as we are. But they won't believe in our discovery! How best can we convince them of the truth?'

'So far you have only mentioned it to high officials who are afraid to venture,' the Presence answered. 'They do not represent the people themselves. I shall not solve your problem for you. That is your own task. Let the *people* know! If you succeed, we shall see what you make of your discoveries — and achievements.'

Abruptly that sense of immense power relaxed. The Presence, whatever it had been, had gone.

Brooks gave himself a little shake and rubbed his forehead.

'Mind!' he breathed, looking at the awe-stricken faces of his sister and Douglas. 'Mind of the *nth* degree! To think that we might have been like that if our ancestors had not been traitors!'

'Or we might have been on Mars as lesser strata,' Douglas pointed out.

'Vera might,' Brooks corrected. 'There has been a cleavage between the highly intelligent and the average type of being. One set has evolved into the highest of intelligences, so much so they are merged into a single unit. The other type has simply become highly evolved humanity with the heights still to be scaled.'

Vera's voice was bitter. 'To which I would belong?' she asked.

'You are not an intellectual, my dear,' Brooks explained, getting to his feet. 'I am. So is Douglas, even if we do have our different outlooks.'

160

Vera hesitated over saying something further, then she changed her mind. In any case her brother had already forgotten his observations. He was pacing up and down, pondering.

'You realize that we have entire *carte blanche* here to do as we wish?' he said at last, coming to a halt. 'We have only to master all there is in this place to gain for ourselves the keys of an even greater kingdom of science. That would mean travel beyond this world, large though it is four-dimensionally. It might even mean the chance to become pure intellectuals. We could travel space without recourse to rocket-driven space machines, as this Presence does. We could reach the furthermost deeps.'

He stopped, recovering a hold of his imagination.

'This city has got to be built again,' he decided. 'And we must have labor to do it. It will need one person, maybe several, for each machine. It will need a directing, guiding mind, too.'

'We know all that,' Vera sighed. 'But how are you ever going to tell the people?

We shan't return to our own plane for a long time yet, and even when we do nobody will believe us.'

'No,' Brooks agreed, frowning thoughtfully. 'Yet there must be a way. I'll think of something, eventually. Tomorrow I resume my study of the machines. Maybe I'll find an instrument somewhere, which will give me an idea. Right now I think our best move is to get to bed.'

The following morning Mason Brooks started his second analysis of the machines with a new zest. He also now had the advantage of seeing each machine operate since the central power-disseminating tower constantly radiated its energy.

Each machine he tested he noted down in detail, deciding later upon its precise function. Douglas and Vera accompanied him on his travels, especially into the more distant machine room, but he missed that hidden lever slot with the stone over it.

Ultimately he came back to the main hall where they had made their headquarters and concentrated his attention on the device that had operated at first when they had crossed the field of the electric eyes. How the thought impressions had been made, and the paralysis created while sensory impressions prevailed, he had not the least idea, but there was a simpler side to the apparatus that claimed his attention.

After a whole day of studying the instrument he explained what was in his mind.

'This thing has a central transmitting plate,' he said, as Douglas and Vera studied it. 'You see this wafer-thin disk inside the protective casing? Its metal is similar to that comprising the energy-absorbing globe on the tower top there. Atomic setup is slightly different, though, meaning it is tuned for far lesser vibrations than the tower ball.

'Those lesser vibrations, I believe, are thought-waves. Thought-waves have a definite vibration, remember — slight though it is. This disk captures them, and the energy thereof is passed into the transformers, and out from this antenna here. When the scientists left their

163

thought message, they did it simply by leaving a thought-record, as we might a phonograph disk. But with it they added sensory impression vibrations, which belongs to this complicated mass of machinery down here.

'That part I don't understand yet. It might take me years to grasp the secret. But I do realize that this machine, as it is, with the sensory impression part cut out of circuit, can amplify thought.'

'And how much good does that do us?' Vera asked.

'It brings us the people we need,' Brooks said slowly. A complacent grin spread over his face. 'Thought waves, by all the laws of science, are not stopped by any solid, any distance, or any dimension. That being so they will pass — amplified remember — from this into our own plane. We can force anybody we wish to come here!'

'Hypnotically?' Douglas questioned.

The scientist made an impatient gesture.

'Of course. But let me finish. We need quite a lot of people here to help us, and it might take a long time to get them individually. So I suggest that famous men and women of our own plane should be forced hypnotically to tell the people what we have here. Vera, with her double sight, can see exactly where such people are. Unknown to them, we can focus this machine right on them, compel them to do whatever we wish.

'The City Scientists can force Congress to grant money for the building of 'transition' machines. And if that doesn't work, I'll order the President himself to do it. In a word I'll twist those confounded obstinate higher-ups around my little finger!' Brooks' mouth had set harshly.

Douglas nodded. 'Yes, I suppose the thing is scientifically possible,' he agreed. 'In fact it is the only way you will ever start to convince people and get them here. But when they do get here, what then? I recall a rather grandiose scheme of yours to make each one the master of his own machine while you sit in the middle of the web and pool the knowledge of the lot. Is that still your idea?'

'Partly,' Brooks assented. 'At first it will have to be that way. At least until the city is rebuilt. After that — we'll see.'

'Why don't you get the people here and then ask them what shall be done?' Vera suggested. 'That's democratic. By assuming too much power you may come a cropper.'

'I have spent many weeks learning the details of this place,' Brooks answered in grim tones. 'I don't intend to trade my knowledge with a mass of uneducated rabble. Some scientists will come too, I'm hoping, but they'll be in the minority.

'While I understand as much as I do, I'm staying in control. As a scientist the idea of handing over a heritage does not appeal to me. It would bring utter chaos.'

There was a silence before Douglas answered.

'Well, we can see how it works, anyway. When do you propose to start?'

'That is up to Vera.' Brooks glanced at her. 'You know the most famous people in New York as well as I do. If necessary, we'll move to the area of Washington to tackle the President. The one I'd like to

166

get at is that old diehard Walbrook Dean. He speaks every week, weather permitting, in the open park at the back of the Science Institute and gives a lecture on physics. That would be a grand chance. You can see him if he's outside, but not if he's inside a building.'

'What you want me to do then is keep a check on every person of importance able to sway the people, and you go to work when they decide to give an outside address?' the girl asked.

'You have it exactly. Being early summer most of the public addresses, scientific and political, are given in the open air and that's going to help our cause a lot. So, Sis, keep your eyes open.'

'I will,' she promised, and stared beyond the immediate ruin of the hall into the dim, misty outlines of New York itself. She had grown so accustomed to two places at once that her mind had come to discount one and concentrate on the other. But now that she realized she had a task to perform, she began to take her 'mirage' bearings. As near as she could tell she was about half a mile from

Fifth Avenue in an easterly direction.

'If, of course, there should be trouble between these people and ourselves when they arrive, I have many ways of making them do as I wish,' Brooks remarked, thinking. 'Not necessarily thought compulsion, but a display of force. Nothing like it to cow the lesser type of mind.'

'Meaning?' Douglas asked ominously.

'I've examined the ruined hall where you and Vera saw that electronic machine she described to me,' Mason Brooks said. 'Everything in that hall — excepting the electronic machine — is made for warfare. It's an arsenal. Or did you think those things with lenses were limelights?' The physicist gave a cynical laugh.

'I didn't know what they were,' Douglas confessed. 'I guessed the place was military, though.'

'It's a dream of power!' Brooks declared, clenching his fist. 'Any crisis from anywhere could be weathered with machines like those. There are six different sets of radiation-projectors to start with. As near as I can tell, they emit freezing-beams, which stop molecules dead and produce an absolute zero; heat-beams — exciting matter into disintegration; paralyzing beams for fixing a living being utterly rigid; and three others which incorporate atomic energy. For all of them there is a master-switchboard and their range is infinity, near as I can figure. Just as well to know, in case of trouble.'

'You're not thinking of using such horrible things on our own people?' Vera asked blankly, turning.

'Of course not — just so long as they behave!'

The girl moved forward, laid a hand on her brother's arm.

'Are you really trying to set yourself up as a ten-cent dictator?' she asked slowly. 'If I thought for a moment you were, I'd never tell you what I can see in our own plane. That would spoil your plan right from the start!'

'This is absurd!' he protested. 'Just because I point out that we have the wherewithal to protect ourselves, you start to jump to conclusions.'

For a long moment the girl hesitated, searching his keen gray eyes. She was not quite sure what she read there but, woman-like, she decided he was entitled to the benefit of her doubt.

'All right,' she said quietly. 'Only don't stride too far! I haven't forgotten what the Presence said, you know. We can only take over in earnest if we prove worthy. Bullying isn't the way to do it.'

Brooks grinned and patted her arm. 'I'll be a good boy, Sis. I promise!'

12

Journey for 2,000

More than a week elapsed before Vera discovered the first subject for the thought amplification experiment, and during that week her ever-active brother had discovered something else. The radio equipment was capable, on its ultra short length, of receiving, but not transmitting, the radio waves disseminated in the normal three planes. There was a slight distortion due to its journey through the narrow veil of vibration separating the two planes, but it was still understandable.

Exactly how it was done was a problem upon which Brooks intended to exercise his mind in the future. Being a good scientist, he was content to accept the genius of the master race for what it was without giving himself a headache inquiring into the cause.

The discovery gave him an immediate advantage. It would now be possible to keep a finger on the pulse of opinion in their own plane. They would be able to judge exactly how the experiment was making out.

When Vera announced that she had read a poster on a street intersection to the effect that Senator Goldman would make a speech on world economics at the International Air-way Park three evenings later, Brooks immediately went into action and moved his apparatus to the spot where, in the normal plane, the senator would stand on the raised platform. Since the instrument was self-powered it did not matter where it went, and as near as Brooks could judge it would be standing just behind the spot where the senator would be speaking.

Sure enough, on the chosen evening, Vera announced that he was present on the platform, a microphone before him and a quite respectably large audience spread out in the open space willing to while away an hour listening to him.

Mason Brooks had made every preparation. He had put Douglas in charge of the radio, whereby the words of the senator would be relayed from the third plane broadcasting station. An extension from the radio equipment and a subsidiary speaker standing on the rough plain nearby was all Brooks needed. With Vera at his side peering into apparent emptiness he waited for her signals. Then when she gave them, he concentrated.

The effect was immediate, the contact being so close through the veil. In fact the machine did all that was required of it so perfectly that the physicist found time to be surprised.

' . . . and I shall cover the field of economics,' boomed the senator's well-fed voice over the plain, as Douglas tuned him in. 'It is a wide field indeed.' He paused as he received the impact of Brooks' thought-waves. 'A very wide field — but there is a much larger one! And that is the fourth dimension. An entire new world in the fourth dimension was recently discovered by the eminent scientist, Mason Brooks.'

A roar from the assembled people betrayed their surprise.

'It will come as a surprise to you to know that our learned City Scientists hushed up this mighty discovery for fear it might prove a threat to their personal power. They even called their chief physicist, Mr. Brooks, a liar. To show his contempt, Brooks went back into the fourth dimension! I, myself, know of the marvels of this plane, this world we should really all possess.

'There is a way to reach it too, and I can describe the exact machinery needed for the purpose. It is for you, the people, to demand that money and materials become available for such a transit to be made. There is no compulsion about it, of course. Only those among you who are anxious to assert yourselves and demand your rights are now offered the chance.'

Altogether Senator Goldman talked for an hour on the wonders and benefits of the fourth dimension. Though he afterwards vowed that he could not remember a word he had said, the people were more than interested.

At later periods, when they heard the same kind of speech from Walbrook Dean himself, and finally even from the President — for which purpose Brooks and Vera changed their locale in the fourth dimension to match that of Washington in their own world — they became clamorous to know what it was all about.

Goldman had said that he knew how the necessary apparatus could be made, and at the next open air meeting he gave every detail, just as Brooks willed him to do, he himself taking the facts from the electronic machine, for he had never made an actual formula.

The struggle was over then. The people demanded some sort of action, and a somewhat bemused Walbrook Dean, in collaboration with the President, were obliged to give it to them. Four dimensional transit machines were mass-produced and then set up in a specially requisitioned area in Central Park. To many it was considered a stunt and to others an adventure.

Still others, mainly know-it-alls, branded

it as the biggest hoax in creation, until with their own eyes these smart-alecks saw people fade into thin air one by one as the power operated.

In consequence of all this there began to drift into the ruins of the fourth dimension a few scattered, bewildered people, men and women dazed by the journey and the incredible land in which they found themselves.

The sight of Brooks, calm and impersonal, with Douglas and Vera at either side of him, did much to raise their courage again. By degrees they began to understand the magnitude of the thing they had done, and they had no complaints. The calculating physicist had prepared everything beforehand. He had caused the automatic machines to create all the necessary food, bedding, and other vital necessities of life. Shelter was unnecessary, anyway, in this land of eternal calm.

The drifting dozens became hundreds. In a week there were two thousand. The ruins of the giant city were black with travelers from the third plane. Then, as

176

Brooks had calculated, the transition machines on the other side burned themselves out after working at such high pressure.

Arrivals thinned — and finally ceased. Once this happened, he made the position clear. Ordering the people out onto the great expanse of plain one morning he stood on a collapsible stool and began talking to them.

'You came here, my friends, either out of idle curiosity or with the hope of getting something for nothing. You believed you were coming into Paradise, and have found only ruins. Well, you can have that Paradise, if you are prepared to work for it! There is super-science in this crumbled city, which I alone understand.

'If you are prepared to help, a new city can be built, and once that is done you will find yourselves in absolute security with nothing more to worry you and with science ever at your elbow. If you do not feel like work, then reflect that there is no way back! I hold that key.

'The machines which transferred you here gave you enough energy change to keep you here for many years. Periodic recharges on this side can keep you here until death. If you don't wish to work you will find yourselves outcasts in a strange, weird land that you do not understand. But if you do work, under my orders, you can have everything!'

'Then we were brought here by false pretenses!' somebody shouted angrily. 'We were told that science had discovered our rightful heritage and that by claiming it we would find everlasting peace. Even the President took part in the discussion and told us that.'

'The President merely told you what I told him to tell you,' Brooks answered calmly, gazing round. 'That gives you some idea of the enormous power I wield, when even the President is at my behest. It was not a false promise, my friend. I have told you how you achieve peace and comfort — and that is work. As you should. To labor for science is an honor!'

'What do we do then?' demanded a woman in the front of the crowd.

'I have devised a labor-direction bureau,' Brooks answered her. 'It will operate in the main machinery hall. From each of you I will learn of your qualifications and then assign you to the appropriate task. The more brilliant of you, granting there are any, can become teachers and over-seers. I propose to start this indexing after we have lunched in the usual way. For the moment that is all.'

Brooks stepped down and waited for a while, a cold glint in his gray eyes as he saw a rather menacing movement towards him from the body of the crowd. Then, evidently none too sure of how much power he possessed, the people broke up and began to drift back towards the city ruins.

'What's the idea?' Douglas demanded. 'If ever there was an aggressive speech that was it. You're lucky they didn't go for you!'

'They're rabble, as I expected,' Brooks answered. 'I saw each one as they arrived. Not one high-up or scientist amongst them. Ordinary, little people who stick in their own petty ruts from the cradle to the grave, the type who jump at the chance to live for nothing on somebody else's efforts.

'They thought they had found the Promised Land when they arrived here. Now I think I have changed their viewpoint. Had there been any intellectuals, I'd have talked differently, but to a mob like this authority is the only whip. Believe me, I know what I'm doing.'

'Well, I don't like it!' Douglas retorted. 'At least they are entitled to courtesy.'

Brooks' lips became a thin, harsh, merciless line.

'That kind never is,' he answered. His lips set a little. 'And let me tell you something, Doug — and you too, Sis, for that matter. Neither of you realize even now the value of the thing we have in our hands, the hopeless chaos that would ensue without rigid control.

'I've got the labor I need and science of the nth degree. I'm going to use it, mould it, build it, and no silly sense of restraint or idealism, or that cock-and-bull non-sense about a rightful heritage, is going to stop me.'

With that he turned away decisively

and began to strut in apparent seven-leagued strides towards the city ruins.

'I think we had a good idea when we concealed the truth about that underground arsenal,' Douglas said thoughtfully, gazing after him.

'That makes two of us!' Vera's voice was angry. 'He's behaving like an idiot!'

'Not an idiot, dearest. He's too clever a man for that. He simply realizes that he has tremendous power and means to use it. That has been the failing of ambitious men down all the ages. He has got to be stopped, if only for his own good. You and I have a say in this, too. We were in at the beginning.'

'But since he gives the orders and has all the science, what can we do?'

'I don't know yet, but my original idea of the people coming here to work out their destiny as they wish, leisurely and with mutual understanding of the problems, has got to come about somehow even if I have to use force to make this aggressive brother of yours see sense. Well, that's ahead of us. Can't do anything right now except have dinner. Come on.'

13

The Widening Rift

Discontented applicants soon learned Mason Brooks' Labor Direction Bureau consisted of a portable table at which he sat, and a mathematical machine standing on three legs beside him. This astonishing contrivance, powered like most other things from the central tower, noted down every detail of the applicant — height, weight, muscular power, size of brain, intellectual development, and so forth — and within a space of ten seconds delivered a print-out stating exactly what kind of work the applicant should undertake.

The one word 'Driller,' 'Machinist,' 'Welder,' or whatever it might be, was the language of the master race, of course, but with very few exceptions Brooks understood them. He had had plenty of time by now to discover the meaning of single words, though the language as a whole, as he had found it in the records, was highly complex.

Learning the details of the two thousand applicants was a job that took four days in itself, for the name of each had to be recorded by Vera and indexed with details of that person's potential capacity, but the actual assignment of work was far harder.

It took nearly a month of planning on Brooks' part to decide who fitted into what. Finally, though, he managed it and had the satisfaction of knowing that every man and woman was in some way employed in the job of rebuilding the city. There were no wages. It was either work or starve. That more than one of the victims was highly resentful was perfectly obvious.

But the physicist was satisfied. He had nothing to do now but watch the ruins being gradually cleared away and the foundations of a new city being laid. Around the demolished walls of the machine-halls new skeletons were springing up, one person to each marvelous machine, and hundreds of different varieties of apparatus being used. Here, in this process of machine control, Brooks revealed the subtle depths of his plans.

Knowing that concentration by one person on one machine must mean the discovery of every detail concerning the contrivance, he saw to it that a written report was handed in to him each day by each worker about the machine's behavior. So, by degrees, he began to amass a vast quantity of information on each machine's working, for study when time permitted. In other words his old grandiose scheme of each worker not knowing what the other was doing, while he himself mastered the entire setup, was showing signs of a vigorous rebirth.

Douglas, though, was by no means idle. Though he was not actually a worker, he pretended that he had much to do to determine the nature of the instruments in the observatory. From here, away from Brooks in the adjoining main hall, it was only a short trip in the oddly foreshortening distance to that other hall where lay the entrance to the underground arsenal.

Here — when he could be sure he was not being observed — for so far the workers had not started on this section, he brought his rather circumscribed scientific knowledge into play to try and discover how the underground armies were controlled. It took him nearly a dozen visits before he realized that their control was from below and had nothing to do with the switchboards above.

This revelation, and the discovery that the floor trap could also be shut by a counter-lever from below, gave him satisfaction. If ever he needed to use this mighty army to curb Brooks' too high-flown ambitions, he could do it safely, out of sight in the underworld, only opening the trap when he was ready to attack. Had it been otherwise it would have been impossible for the upper hall contained, of course, all the other deadly sources of attack of which Brooks was fully aware.

To find that the control was below, and to know how it worked, were two different things, though. Whenever he could, Douglas took Vera with him and together, the trap closed behind them, they spent odd hours deciding which switch controlled a certain area or machine.

They had light too to work by, for since the advent of the central power tower cold light globes had come into being, drenching the remotest corners of the underworld in shadowless brilliance.

Indeed the place was so enormous that it took them many weeks to determine fully its extent, and in the process they found that it harbored even more things than robots, planes, and tanks. There were also queerly-fashioned guns, screen-projectors which Douglas assumed would emit radiant energy, and in one depart-ment were hundreds upon hundreds of metal cases filled with tiny gray ovoids fitted with detonator caps. They could only be bombs, and from their smallness presumably utilized the shattering power of atomic force.

At the furthest extremity of the immense cavity they discovered yet another opening in the roof, to which the floor rose gently. A lever shifted the trap and they emerged to find themselves in open plain near the sea, the city ruins so far away in measureless distance that they were out of sight.

'This is just what we want,' Douglas declared, on the morning they made this discovery. 'Mason can never interfere with us if we keep this a secret. Obviously the city at one time extended even this far, but whatever machines there were here have been removed.'

He pointed to the dusty ruins of collapsed walls, and then to the solitary lever remaining for the trap. It moved clumsily under his efforts. He had to shift it back and forth several times before there was any ease of movement. Then, as in the case of the previous lever he had found, he unscrewed it and hid it beneath a distinctive piece of masonry.

'You seem to be pretty pessimistic over Mace's ambitions,' the girl remarked presently, as they began to walk slowly in the direction of the distant city ruins.

'Can you blame me? He's revealed exactly what he intends to do, and I just don't intend to allow him. We may come to blows over our varying policies finally, and I'm not deluding myself into thinking that he'll be content with mere words to prove he is right.

'Mason will probably use force. If so, I intend to be ready for him. I'm more glad than I can say that we've found this secret entrance to below. We'll never be interfered with, and we can throw away the lever controlling the other entrance. In time we'll figure out how all that other underground stuff works.'

'Yes, I suppose it's the only course,' the girl admitted. 'Funny thing how you men always want to start fighting. You won't believe this, I suppose, but all I really want is to go back home, have my eyes put right, and live like a normal girl with millions in the bank. This place doesn't interest me a bit. It's too fantastic, too diabolically clever!'

Douglas smiled and gripped her arm gently.

'I'll fix your eyes yet. I give you my word. Either here — or back home. All depending on which way the wind blows.'

With the passing of eight weeks

Douglas had the time, with Vera's assistance, to solve the problems of the arsenal. Hard study and trial and error showed him how to make the robots move, how to control their weapons, how to pilot the airplanes and drive the tanks, how to operate the radiant-energy screens.

The inner forces controlling them he did not understand, but the matter of maneuver and mobility was no more difficult than guiding an automobile in a given direction, once he got the hang of the remote-control panels.

Since the panels possessed television eyes, which in turn recorded the exact movements of every robot, tank, and plane he felt he could, if the grim necessity arose, handle a whole war from a sitting position before the switchboards.

He said not a word to Mason Brooks needless to say, and neither did Vera. In fact the physicist was too absorbed in his own affair to be much concerned with other activities anyway. One day, however, he must have wondered how they spent their time for as they sat at dinner in the rebuilt building they had made their headquarters he asked a question.

'Taking you a long time to find out what the lenses and instruments in the observatory are for, isn't it, Doug?'

'My science doesn't equal yours,' Douglas answered. 'In any case I am not devoting myself to it exclusively. I've been doing lot of thinking, trying to plan out a new pair of eyes for Vera here. She can't go on with double vision indefinitely.'

'No, I suppose not.' The physicist reflected for a moment. 'But why try and devise a pair of normal eyes? Why not a pair modeled on the style of the fourth-dimensional eyes our ancestors possessed, using the *plica semi-lunaris* in its full range?

'Think of what that would mean! Vera would be the first human being since the Outcasts to understand this plane properly to see it as it should be seen.'

'It's I — your sister — you're talking about!' the girl objected. 'I'm just reminding you in case you think I'm a guinea pig.'

Brooks raised his eyebrows in surprise.

'But you want to help, don't you? Since another operation will have to come sooner or later it may as well be to some purpose. What is the use of having just a pair of ordinary eyes? You'll be as blind as the rest of us to the fourth dimension's real meaning; On the other hand, with the change, you could become really useful.

'As it stands, your only usefulness lies in being able to see two planes at once, but as we grow in power here that won't be a necessity. After the operation, you can occupy a really high position by being a genuine four-dimensional-eyed woman.'

The girl did not say anything. It was obvious that her brother's utter disregard for her feelings had shocked her.

'I am not going to make such a pair of eyes, either for the sake of your ambition, or any other reason,' Douglas said in a level voice. 'Even if I *could* make them, which is next to impossible without drawn specifications or at least a close study of the lenses involved.

'Vera is going to have normal sight, the same as you or I. And in case you've forgotten it, I'm intending to marry a normal, very attractive girl and not a scientific freak doomed to work herself to a frazzle just to further your ends.'

Brooks grinned.

'Okay. That's plain speaking. It's the way I like it. I confess though that I don't understand why you throw away such golden opportunities. Personally I would never marry an ornament —'

He got to his feet and flexed his capable hands.

'Well, work to be done,' he said. 'We're getting this city very nicely into shape, even if I do have trouble at times.'

'Trouble?' Vera questioned. 'What trouble?'

'If you stayed around to help instead of wandering God knows where, you'd find out! One or two workers — men, and bone idle — have been slacking on the job. I had to give them a dose of paralysis to warn them. Unpleasant for them to have every muscle locked tighter than an atomic system, of course, but they asked for it. They've come to heel since. Well, I've got to be off.'

He turned to the door, then stopped as Douglas jumped up and caught his arm.

'Wait a minute, Mason!' There was a grim hardness in Douglas' face that made the physicist elevate an eyebrow. 'I don't think I heard you aright. Do you mean to say you punished those poor devils with paralyzing machines?'

'I do,' Brooks assented coldly. 'Any objections? Or have you forgotten that I'm the boss here?'

'I haven't forgotten anything, but I realize that with so much power around you, you are in danger of losing your head. If you start punishing people in that way, there'll be a revolution.'

'I should worry.' Brooks shrugged. Then withdrawing himself from Douglas' grip, he added, 'Do me a favor, Doug, and concentrate on your own job. I'll handle my own affairs.' He turned and went out, but struck with sudden thought Douglas again stopped him.

'I'm stuck for labor,' he explained, as the physicist came back to his side. 'I can't work out all the details of the observatory without assistance.'

'Then why didn't you ask for it before?' Brooks demanded. 'You can have fifty, a hundred, two hundred men or women if you want.'

'A hundred men and a hundred women will suffice,' Douglas said, thinking.

'Okay, I'll have them report at the observatory ruins in thirty minutes, and see that you keep them up to their work.'

With a nod Brooks went on his way at last towards the dark mass of workers swarming over the masonry of the newly rising city. Douglas looked after him. He turned as Vera came to his side.

'What on earth do you want labor for?' she asked curiously.

'Because there's trouble coming,' he muttered. 'I'm going to take one last chance and try and show Mason where he's wrong. I intend to treat the people who work for me as human beings. They will be bound to tell the folks who work for Mason and that will start comparisons and maybe bring things to a head. Mason will then either have to climb down, or — '

He left his sentence unfinished and caught the girl's arm.

'We'd better get over to the observatory

and deal with the people as they come.'

In silence they went across to the twin buildings of machine hall and observatory. On the way they passed Brooks in the midst of his workers, giving sharp instructions. Already a file of men and women was moving towards the adjoining observatory. By the time they had arrived Douglas and the girl were in position by the telescope, awaiting them.

Douglas made a note of each one's capabilities and then surveyed them as they stood waiting. He could not help but notice the signs of strain and overwork on their faces.

'All you have to do, is study each machine and instrument here and see what use you can make of it,' he said quietly. 'When you have found out all you know let me have your reports.'

'How long have we got?' asked one of the men in a grim voice.

'There's no time limit,' Douglas told him. 'Nothing worth while can be learned in a hurry.'

The men and women glanced at each other in surprise.

'But Mr. Brooks sets a time limit on everything we do,' one of the women remarked. 'If it isn't done in that time he gives the women extra work, or else punishes the men.'

'You are not answerable to Brooks here,' Douglas replied. 'I am in sole charge of this section.'

Then he turned away deliberately. The men and women looked around them, obviously a little dazed by their unexpected good fortune. After a while they began to work on the machine or instrument nearest to hand.

For half an hour Douglas watched them tacitly, Vera beside him, then he said in a low voice:

'You take the folks on the left. I'll take those on the right. Talk to them. Let them see we value them. Give them cooperation as they've never known it since they came here.'

'Right,' the girl agreed, and then off she went.

Douglas turned to the other side of the room and stopped beside an elderly man who was thoughtfully studying a spectroheliograph.

'Everything okay?' he asked, with a pleasant smile.

'Eh?' The man started nervously. Then in a quick voice he answered. 'Yes, yes, sir — everything's okay. I'm not very quick at my age, I'm afraid. This is a bit different to watch making.'

'Take it easy,' Douglas interrupted. 'No hurry remember.'

The man relaxed.

'I'd — I'd forgotten. You're so different to Mr. Brooks. He's very — well strict. Not easy to forget it.'

'You will,' Douglas assured him, and moved on to the next worker . . .

14

The Presence Returns

Questioning them in a leisurely fashion, Douglas had a word with all of them on the right hand side of the observatory. This done, he left them all to their own devices and went for his usual visit, with Vera, to the underground arsenal. When they returned they found the workers lined up with their reports, waiting to be received and checked out.

Douglas took each report with a nod of thanks. When he had finally been handed the last report one of the men spoke up.

'I'd like to thank you, Dr. Ashfield, for the way you've been treating us. I'm speaking for all of us here. If there was the same fair-mindedness elsewhere, this plane wouldn't be such a bad place after all.'

'The remedy is in your own hands,' Douglas answered quietly. 'If you don't like Mr. Brooks' way of doing things, tell him so! I'll back you up.'

'That's good hearing, sir, but — well, I'm afraid Mr. Brooks has ways of enforcing his wishes. He's got scientific instruments which can crush any objections by force.'

'I still say I'll back you up,' Douglas replied. 'You don't have to object immediately. Wait until you have a really good reason. Until then, you'll be working for me here. If you can get others to work here as well, all to the good. You'll receive fair treatment.'

The man nodded gratefully and turned away with the men and women about him. Evidently he had given matters some thought too for the next day a hundred more workers reported for duty. At this number, however, Brooks put his foot down and no more were forthcoming. So for a week at least, all seemed to go quite smoothly without any signs of friction from the workers under Brooks' direct control, though all of them knew by now that he was the sole reason why fear and lack of cooperation were present.

There were, of course, certain spirits who agreed with him in his methods — or else it was that they were smart enough to play along with him in the hope of getting something out of it later. These few he placed in charge of small groups and the consequent relaxation of labor for them was just what they wanted.

Then came the breaking point. Douglas and Vera, in the observatory, were busy amongst their own team of workers one morning when the noise of angry voices from somewhere outside reached them. They had hardly moved towards the observatory's outer door before a woman worker came dashing in, her eyes wild in fright, blood welling from a vicious cut across her face.

'Doctor Ashfield — Sir! Please! Help me!'

She caught imploringly at his arm and then took refuge behind him as a woman entered the observatory abruptly, a short-nosed whip with a fine metal lash in her hand.

'Don't let her hit me again!'

The woman squeezed herself against

Douglas, covered her bleeding face with her hand.

Douglas put a reassuring arm about her shoulders, then turned to face the female guard who came slowly to a halt, her square face set hard.

'I'm sorry this had to happen, Dr. Ashfield,' she said briefly. 'This woman went crazy and dashed away. She had no right to bother you with her nonsense.'

'She had every right — and you are trespassing on my territory!' Douglas retorted. 'Leave at once!'

The woman half turned then paused as there came a sudden surge of workers through the doorway, their shouts clearly showing their anger. Before Douglas could do a thing to prevent it they had seized the woman guard in their midst and bundled her outside.

'They'll lynch her,' Vera gasped.

Douglas thrust the injured woman into the girl's arms and dived for the doorway. By sheer main strength he fought his way to the center of the disturbance where the female guard lay on the ground, her clothes torn, her face and neck scratched and cut. With a jerk Douglas got her on her feet. Then Brooks himself came pushing through the crowd.

'What's going on here?' he demanded, glaring round. Then at the sight of the woman he gave a start. 'They did this to you?'

'And with good reason,' a man retorted hotly. 'She hit my wife across the face with that whip of hers. I saw her do it. This sort of thing has gone far enough. We're quitting!'

Brooks looked about him, pale-faced, his lips tight. Then he turned as from the observatory came the whipped woman herself, blood oozing from the cut on her face. Vera helped her gently forward. Behind them came the workers under Douglas' control.

'You're getting things into a nice mess with your force policy, Mason,' Douglas snapped. 'It's got to stop!'

'Oh?' Brooks smiled bitterly. 'It's got to stop, has it?'

'What do you other workers stay with this slave-driver for?' shouted the elderly man who'd been a watchmaker. 'Work for

Doctor Ashfield here and get yourselves a square deal!'

There came a grumble of rage from the gathered people. Brooks glared round on them.

'Because a woman guard has been over-zealous is no reason for such hostility,' he shouted. 'I've only been firm in my rules for the common good.'

'Aw, shut up! We're not working for any tinhorn dictator any more!'

There were surgings and movements in the crowd. Brooks stood his ground, and nobody attacked him directly though they came dangerously close. Soon even he could see that all but perhaps a hundred or so of the workers drifted over to the spot where Douglas and Vera were standing.

'This is very interesting,' Brooks said at last, trying hard to keep his fury under restraint. 'Out of some two thousand people I have a hundred left who are loyal to me! I suppose you think, Douglas — and you too, Sis — that this is a resounding triumph for your precious policy of share-and-share-alike?'

'It's a triumph for ordinary decent people who refuse to be kicked around, anyway,' Vera answered candidly.

The physicist looked at the grim-faced men and women who had elected to stay with him, chiefly because they knew just how much power he could wield when necessary.

He gave a cold smile.

'I never thought that when we set out to rebuild this city it would come to a parting of the ways,' he said. 'Since it has to be I'm not shirking the issue. In a scheme as huge as this there just can't be two masters. It has either got to be run my way — or yours, and the people must follow the victor.'

'How do you propose to put it to the test?' Douglas snapped.

'You'll see! You know I have the means of making my will obtain. You have nothing but some one thousand nine hundred men and women who won't be able to stand five seconds against scientific destruction.'

Brooks paused and reflected for a moment. Then his mouth set harshly.

'I'll give you until ten tonight, Douglas, to think things over. By that time you workers must come back to me, and your infraction will be overlooked. If you don't come back I'll give you such a terrible time you'll finally come crawling on your bended knees.'

He turned away with an impatient movement and went striding off to the small headquarters building with his hundred devotees trailing after him.

Around Douglas and Vera a silence dropped, save for the self-piteous sniffing of the woman who had been whipped.

'You'll help us, I suppose?' the woman's husband asked bluntly.

'How can he?' demanded another. 'Brooks has all the science. Best thing we can do is wreck the machinery and stop him that way.'

'You can't wreck machines like these,' Douglas said quietly. 'They are foolproof. But I gave you my word I would stand behind you and I meant just that.

'I want you all to go to your home sites and collect provisions for about three days. Then this afternoon you will join

Miss Brooks and myself on that plain over there. I have a surprise for you. Since force against force is the only answer to this deadlock so it must be. So — we meet again this afternoon . . . '

Mason Brooks' belief in his own rightness — and therefore his complete disregard for the movements of the renegade workers during the afternoon — lost him the chance of observing what happened to them. He certainly noted the general exodus towards the plain in the dim distance, but since watching them was like gazing through the wrong end of a telescope he ceased to be interested in them.

Towards four o'clock he had made an end of his plans to deal with the situation if agreement was not forthcoming, and his first act was to look towards the plain. He beheld not a single trace of the workers who had been just visible as a remotely distant blur of black.

For an instant suspicion crossed his mind, and then faded. The most likely explanation was that they had all run for it. In that case they would be back, and forced to heel. So he spent the rest of the late afternoon and evening showing his hundred followers how to operate the various ray-projectors and weapons of destruction in the armament hall.

'With these we can deal with any emergency,' he explained. 'I will give the order when to use them, and it will only be in the event of genuine attack. I want every worker I can get who is willing to return. This confounded strike has upset my schedule!'

On this note he left the matter and waited, consulting his watch at intervals.

Far below him, a mile and more, the workers who had followed Douglas and Vera were getting over their first pleasurable shock of discovering a mighty armament dump at their disposal and were learning how the robots, planes, tanks and projectors worked.

'Not that I like any of it,' Douglas confessed, as his watch showed it was seven o'clock in the evening. 'But if it has to be civil war, that is the end of it. Mason Brooks is one of those kind of men who is not willfully vicious but misguidedly ambitious. He's got to learn — by hard knocks. And at ten o'clock we'll show him.'

The workers in the huge cavern murmured an assent. Then at Douglas' order, they settled down to a meal. In this manner another hour passed. From that time on until ten o'clock was a period of intense mental strain for Douglas. He realized that many things might happen.

He might make mistakes in controlling the huge robot system of warfare. Or, to spike his guns, Brooks might cut the power of the central tower and thereby bring things to a halt. But since Brooks didn't know what was afoot anyway, and because stoppage of power would queer his own plans, too, this didn't seem a likely possibility.

The only thing was to chance it. At five to ten Douglas made the first moves. He had the trap opened onto the plain, and he sat by the switchboard in readiness to throw the master control. Vera was beside him, and stretching back into the distances, alert and intent, were the workers.

The second hand of his watch clicked round — 9:56 . . . 9:58 . . . 9:59 . . .

'Okay!' he snapped.

He waited, but nothing happened. He found himself gazing at dial needles that had dropped to zero on their scales.

A second or two later, the lights in the hall went out and left only that dim oblong open to the starry sky about two miles away. The big heating grids against the walls were paling into pink bars and thence fading into blackness.

The silence was intense for a moment, a silence born of utter surprise and disappointment. Then shouts came out of the dark.

'The power's off!'

'This is Brooks' doing!'

'He's found out about us!'

Douglas sat trying to reason the mystery out. He felt Vera pressing against him as the people surged forward past her into the open air.

'Can't see how he could have found out,' Douglas said at last, puzzled. 'Nor can I imagine why he'd cut the power and so kill his own chances. We'd better get

209

outside and see what's going on.'

He got up and with difficulty found his way along the aisle to the slope leading to the oblong opening. Vera clung to his arm, and the people, chattering and arguing among themselves, followed him out under the fantastic stars.

In the dim distances across the plain the ruins of the city were utterly black. This in itself was unusual since it had been Brooks' practice, since the restoration of power, to have the powerful lights blazing from all sides.

'May be a trick,' Vera warned. 'Better take it easy.'

'We'll all stick together and head for the city,' Douglas decided. 'Come on.'

They began to advance slowly in a tightly packed body, but before they had covered half the distance under the uncertain starlight, a black mass loomed ahead of them, and with the suddenness characteristic of this weird place it merged into Mason Brooks himself and his hundred satellites.

'That you, Douglas?'

His sharp, authoritative voice floated

out of the gloom as both parties paused expectantly.

'Yes,' Douglas assented. 'What have you done to the power?'

'The power? What should you need power for?'

Douglas was silent for a second or two. He had forgotten that the physicist knew nothing of the arsenal. It was Vera who spoke next and cleared up the uncertainty.

'We needed power for a robot army to teach you a much needed lesson, Mace. Just as we were about to use it, the power failed.'

Brooks came forward in the gloom until Douglas and Vera could faintly discern his features.

'So you had a robot army, eh? So that was where you vanished to. I guess you must have been smarter than I imagined. Well, it didn't do you much good, did it? And I didn't cut off the power either. I was all prepared with my defensive weapons to ward off whatever you sent against me — and I only expected workers — but nothing worked and the

211

lights went out! Not a single power unit is in action, not even the self-powered machines. Even batteries have gone flat.'

'All power couldn't just fade out like this,' Douglas protested, as mutual antagonism was forgotten for the moment in face of this major problem. 'It must have — '

He could not finish his sentence for he was drowned out by a sudden cry from a woman in the gathered hundred behind Brooks.

'The sky!' she shrieked. 'Look!'

Every eye gazed upwards, and in spite of himself Douglas felt a curious little thrill pass through him. Something wraith-like, as impalpable as the Milky Way, was curling like vapor out of the depths of space. It swept earthwards with an incredible velocity, blotting out the stars for a moment . . . Then upon every one of the watching people settled a sudden and immovable paralysis, the crushing load of a supermind probing into every brain.

'Fools! Descendants of fools!' the voice of the Presence came to their consciousness. 'In thousands of years of evolution you have not even yet learned how to handle the powers of science. Idiots! Little brains! You had the keys of infinite progress in your hands. You were rebuilding the city — albeit not entirely by methods which met with our approval — and then what? You disagreed. You forgot your aims, forgot everything, suddenly realized you must use scientific power to destroy each other so that one or other of you could rule.

'You, Mason Brooks, were the cause of that. But to single you out as the prime criminal would be pointless. All of you are to blame — squabbling, fighting, preparing to destroy machinery which it took cycles of careful thought to create, all so you might assert your own miserable, petty wills.'

The scathing bitterness of the mental voice had such power behind it that it wrenched every nerve and organ. It went on:

'We decided that you should not be allowed to do it. You are not fitted to inherit this great four-dimensional plane with its mighty scientific secrets. You have

213

much yet to learn before you can even approach the attainments of the lowly people of the world you call Mars.

'You are but barbarians who have many generations of refinement to undergo before you can even hope to be admitted into the anteroom of the vast universe we hold in trust for you. Yes, we decided that you are unworthy.

'We placed a negative influence over the machines. Mind is ever the master of matter, electrical forces, and elemental powers. We willed that not a single machine should work, that power be taken from you.'

Again the pause and the dreadful silence indicative of vaster thoughts to come.

'You have failed. You will have to learn how to defeat greed, personal power, mad ambition, before you are even worthy to move a single power switch in this plane. Bereft of power you could die here, but that is not our wish.

'We have decided that you shall be returned to your own plane, there to remain until sense, and the refinement of centuries teaches you to handle an exquisite gift with reverent care.'

The voice ceased — but the sense of paralysis increased to awful, crushing proportions. The people cried out in sudden anguish. Douglas felt Vera clinging to him. He could hear Brooks cursing the Presence huskily.

Then suddenly there was a blaze of light that seemed to consume the universe. At the same moment the ground shook under the impact of a myriad of thunders. There was a mighty rush of air, a blast of intolerable heat. Douglas went flying through emptiness to land on his face with a mighty detonation roaring in his ears . . .

15

Eyes Without Vision

Hours later, Douglas found himself lying amidst rubble and broken stone, pieces of debris falling upon him even as he stirred. For a second or two he hardly moved. After a while the distant sound of ambulance or fire engine sirens came to him and he made an effort and looked about him.

He gave a violent start. At a distance were the gleaming lights of New York's familiar buildings, but around him for an area of nearly two square miles there was a shambles of fallen stone, crumbling plastic walls, and fantastically twisted girders. An explosion of inconceivable power had occurred.

As he clambered unsteadily to his feet he could see other people getting up too, moving bewilderedly, trying to find out where they were. A hand gripped him. It was Brooks, his pale face streaked with dirt and blood, his usually immaculate hair hanging lankly about his forehead.

'Where's Vera?' he demanded hoarsely. 'Help me find her.'

Douglas did not need to be asked twice. Nor did they have to search for long by themselves. The ambulances and fire engines were soon on the spot, and with them came a huge army of sightseers who gazed wonderingly in the light of the hastily erected floodlamps upon a battered, bruised and confused file of survivors being interrogated by the police.

Ignoring all the commotion about them, Douglas and Brooks kept close to each other, here and there coming across a dead body, here and there releasing an injured man or woman. When this happened they called an ambulance man to take charge of the victim.

At last they discovered the figure they sought for, sprawled on her back amidst the fallen girder work and stone. Fortunately Vera was not buried, but she had certainly been badly mauled. Her clothes were torn, one arm was lacerated, and —

'Good Heavens!' Douglas whispered, as the floodlight caught her face and the ambulance men came up. 'Look!'

The physicist stared dumbly. Those extraordinary artificial eyes were splintered — both of them — their lenses powdered irreparably as though they had been hit with a hammer. Neither man spoke — the shock was too great. They watched as the girl was placed on a stretcher and carried away. Then they followed mutely to the ambulance in which she was placed.

They were about to climb in and keep her company to the hospital when a police inspector held them back.

'Particulars from you two gentlemen, if you please. What happened here? Nobody seems to know.' The officer stopped, gazing at Brooks. 'Why, isn't it Mr. Brooks? The man who discovered the fourth dimension?'

'Yes, and the man who got thrown out of it too!' the physicist replied acidly. 'That's what caused this havoc.'

'So that was it! We thought it was a

chemical explosion. The Chemical Institute had storerooms here you know. Two whole blocks of buildings went skywards. Is that your sister on the stretcher there?'

'Yes, and we're going with her.' Brooks turned away impatiently and climbed into the ambulance with Douglas behind him. But, determined to finish the job the inspector followed them into the vehicle.

'This sort of happening takes the shine off things, sir,' he commented, as the ambulance doors were slammed. 'You were all set for being fêted when you returned from the dimension — but after this destruction and loss of life I'm not so sure.'

'Fêted?' The physicist took his troubled eyes from the unconscious girl. 'What the devil for? I was as good as bounced by the City Scientists for my work.'

'Yes, but you proved your words afterwards. Or rather Senator Goldman Walbrook Dean, and even the President did so by means of public speeches. Then we all saw two thousand people melt into the fourth dimension in Central Park. That couldn't be called a trick, sir.

219

Walbrook Dean had to admit the mighty discovery you had made. The President ordered that you be acclaimed a great scientific discoverer when you returned.'

Brooks grinned crookedly.

'Well, I have returned! The rest is up to the people and the law!'

The inspector nodded, took down the particulars Douglas gave about himself. By the time this was furnished, they had reached the city's main hospital. Silently the two men followed the girl's stretcher-bearers directly into the operating theater. This was as far as they were allowed to go. The doctor in charge sent them out into the anteroom once he had made his examination.

'She'll live all right,' he announced. 'At least you have that to be thankful for. Concussion mainly, and that cut arm. Soon fix up those troubles. What worries me chiefly are her eyes. Offhand I'd say she has some peculiar form of cataract, yet on the other hand they look like smashed unbreakable glass. It's most peculiar — '

Douglas interrupted the surgeon. 'I can

explain it. I'm Douglas Ashfield, stricken from the register by the Ophthalmic Council after giving Miss Brooks two artificial eyes. Those are the ones I made for her. Smashed completely, I'm afraid.'

'Ashfield!' The doctor gave a start. 'Why, of course. I remember the case. And I couldn't see why you shouldn't be right. Anyway, you must have been since these are the very eyes.'

'Leave them just as they are,' Douglas instructed. 'No fragments will dislodge into her brain. I've made them incapable of that. Let me know when you have patched her up and restored her to near-normal. The eyes I'll try and fix myself.'

'I'll do that,' the doctor nodded. 'And good luck!'

He turned back into the operating theater and the two men began to walk slowly down the corridor, side by side. They had nearly reached the front exit before Brooks made a comment.

'You know what happened, of course? That explosion?'

'Not exactly. But I imagine the

221

Presence had something to do with it.'

'He — they — it, whatever it was, must have forced both planes to coincide for a brief second, which caused that appalling havoc. In that moment all traces of the four dimensional atomic arrangement of our bodies was altered back to its normal status and we returned here with devastating force.'

'So that was it. Well, what happens now?'

'We go back there at the earliest opportunity, of course.'

They came to the front entrance of the building, and paused.

'You serious?' Douglas demanded.

'Certainly I am. You don't think I'm going to let all that science pass us by, do you? I have the transition machine for doing the job in my laboratory, remember. We'll rest awhile first, and you'll get Vera right again. And don't forget that she must have that double vision again. It's useful. Makes it easy for us to see what's going on in two places. Back we are going, whatever happens.'

They went out into the street and

began to walk towards the city center, regardless of the dried blood on their faces and their filthy appearance. The things that had happened to them had blunted all remembrance of convention. In any case there were not many people about to see them at this hour.

'I suppose that we should go back,' Douglas said, after due reflection. 'But we'll have to act differently when we get there, Mason. Squabbling as we did . . . We spoiled it!'

Brooks gave a faint grin.

'I suppose we did really. But I'm not going to play second fiddle when I do go back. I'll work without labor. I'll get those robots you found to do it. But I am going to have that science! Now let's forget it for a moment and get a bath, something to eat, and then some sleep. We'll tackle things better in the daylight.'

Douglas nodded and they said no more until the Brooks home was reached. The physicist let himself in with his own latchkey and before doing anything else went straight through to his laboratory. He switched on the light and took three paces towards his transition machine — then he stopped dead. Douglas, immediately behind him, paused too and stared fixedly.

The machine was no longer a magnetic device magnificently created, but a burned out hulk of twisted metalwork and shattered wires and tubes.

'What the devil!' Brooks shrieked, and swung round violently just as the manservant entered sleepily in his dressing gown.

'Oh, it's you, Mr. Brooks. I heard sounds.'

'Who's been tampering with this machine?' Brooks raved at him. 'Who's been in here during my absence?'

Jefferson gazed at the ruin and blinked. 'Why, nobody, sir. You gave me those orders. Only you had the key. Maybe that explosion tonight did it.'

'Explosion, rats! Somebody has deliberately wrecked this machine!'

'I — I just don't know, sir.' Jefferson stood awkwardly waiting as Brooks narrowed his eyes sharply.

'Okay, you can go back to bed,' he snapped.

As the man shambled out Brooks eyed Douglas grimly.

'Whom do you suspect?' he asked slowly.

Douglas shrugged.

'At a rough guess — the Presence!'

'Exactly. The Presence! That all-knowing, all-destructive, all-encompassing mass of confounded interfering mind!' Brooks broke off and breathed hard. 'I shall have to build another one, that's all. If this has gone, it's a certainty those others which were used in Central Park have gone, too, even if they didn't burn themselves to scrap metal making the transitions for the two thousand. Yes, Vera can describe one to me, as she did before. Once you have made those eyes for her.'

Douglas' eyebrows went up in surprise. 'You didn't make a formula then?'

'No need. It was described, so I built it. I was too excited to bother with details. Maybe it was silly of me. About these eyes for Sis — How long will it take you?'

'Depends on the damage. Complete eyes would take me ten years. If the damage lies in the synthetic cornea, as I

225

think it does, I can cure it in three weeks.'

'Good!' Brooks clenched his fists. 'The moment she has recovered consciousness, get busy!'

Early the following morning the police were the first callers. They added particulars to those already taken, and from their observations neither Brooks nor Douglas was left in doubt of the fact that they would be held responsible for the explosive catastrophe of the previous night.

Immediate arrest was prevented, however by the special order of Walbrook Dean, who also ordered a thorough search into the scientific implications first. With this purpose in view, he summoned Brooks to his private chambers for an interview.

While Brooks grudgingly complied with the order, Douglas headed for the hospital to see Vera, now fully conscious again. He found her in bed in a private room, her head and lacerated arm bandaged and her health apparently normal again if the vigor of her voice were any guide.

'Doug!' She gripped his arm as he came to the bedside. 'You are not hurt — or so I'm told.'

'So you can't see me?' he asked quietly.

'No. Everything's gray, like a thick, milky mist.'

He gripped her hands tightly.

'Then you can see a grayness?'

'Nothing else. And I can also see variations in light and shade, when somebody blocks the sunlight for a moment. But actual vision has gone. Just — just what does it mean?' she asked, her voice low. 'That I'm blind again?'

'For three weeks or so, yes. The light you can see now shows that only the surface of the cornea has been shattered. The eye apparatus behind it is undamaged. Otherwise it might have taken me ten years to fix it up.'

He felt her give a little shiver.

'What happened exactly?' she asked presently.

As briefly as possible he told her, and added a few words on the destruction of her brother's machine.

'But surely, Doug, Mace isn't *still*

trying to get back to that horrible place?'

'I'm afraid he is, and I can't blame him. In spite of what happened, it is too wonderful a land and far too scientific to be lost. We can go back there, very much humbled, once I've fixed you up with two visions again.'

'Just so that I can start to describe machinery to Mace! I don't want to do it. I want normal eyes and peace of mind! Please!'

'It's a selfish view,' he murmured. 'I have still my own idea of giving everybody their rightful heritage to put into practice, you know. You have your part to play.'

He patted her hand as she remained silent.

'Now I've got to be going,' he said gently. 'I must get to work on those new lenses right away. When you're ready to leave the hospital, I'll see you home. Or else Mason will. He's been called for an interview with Walbrook Dean. That's why he didn't come along with me to see you.'

Soon after Douglas left her. She was

still protesting against Mason's scientific ambitions, however. As he went on his way pensively through the hospital hall, he found his arm suddenly gripped.

'Why, Dr. Hurley!' he said to the man who had stopped him. In some surprise he took Hurley's extended hand and shook it.

The Chairman of the Ophthalmic Council eyed him levelly for a moment.

'Glad to see you again, Ashfield,' he said briefly. 'I've been doing a lot of thinking about that operation you performed on Miss Brooks. That four-dimensional business brought things to the front. Seems to me that, even if you did give her four-dimensional vision, you at least gave her eyes, of sorts. You overcame her blindness.'

'Good of you to admit it,' Douglas commented, uncompromising.

'Oh, I don't blame you for feeling hurt! I've been talking to the head surgeon of this hospital. He came to see me last night after Miss Brooks had been brought in here. He insisted that I come and look at her artificial eyes, despite their

229

damaged state. I did, and — ' the Chairman cleared his throat — 'you did a good job, Ashfield. There's a lot to be said for your courage in throwing away your practice to risk doing it.'

'Just what is all this leading up to?' Douglas asked grimly.

The Chairman of the Ophthalmic Council leaned forward, his face intent.

'This. Can you cure this girl again? Can you fix her up with normal eyes, and not double-visioned ones?'

Douglas was silent for a moment.

'And if I did?'

'If you did, and her eyes responded to every test we could make, we would not only admit you back to the Ophthalmic Council with a public apology, but would also confer on you the highest degrees the council can give. We would also put you in charge of a laboratory specially devoted to the making of Ashfield Synthetic Optics. Your name would rank among the immortals of science.'

Douglas eyed the Chairman pensively and made a quick gesture.

'After all, Ashfield, it means something,

doesn't it? Full restitution! I would not have gone out of my way to find you, as I have this morning, if I did not mean it. I was told at the Brooks' residence that I'd find you here.'

Douglas' mind strayed for a moment to the recollection of that huge power awaiting the human race in the fourth dimension.

He gave a faint smile.

'I cannot guarantee that the eyes will be normal,' he said. 'They may still see in two places at once.'

'That will be a pity for everybody,' Hurley sighed. 'Anyway, do your best and let me know how you get on. When do you start on these optical repairs?'

'Today — the moment I get home.'

'I'll drive you there. My car's outside.'

16

Glory That Was

Oddly enough to Douglas' surprise he found Mason Brooks waiting for him when he reached his home. The physicist was pacing impatiently up and down outside the front door.

'What news?' he asked, as Douglas fished for his key and then slipped it in the lock.

'I can ask you the same thing,' Douglas answered.

Brooks stared after the retreating car, and frowned.

'Was that Hurley of the Ophthalmic Council?'

'It was he all right. Come along in.'

Douglas entered the hall and walked through into the rear room of the house which he used as his own testing department and lens-manufacturing laboratory.

'Hurley has offered me full restitution, honors, and a name in lights,' Douglas said. 'If I can make Vera see again.'

'Funny how we both seem to be bringing these higher-ups to their senses,' the physicist mused. 'Walbrook Dean is quite convinced of the existence of the fourth dimension after what has happened. Or else it is that he's afraid to admit otherwise for fear of public opinion. Those vanishing folk in Central Park apparently made us candidates for an inscription in bronze.'

'So what happened?' Douglas asked.

'I have been reinstated among the City Scientists. Not as the Chief Physicist but as the head of a new department devoted to study of the fourth dimension. At the earliest moment I want to show Walbrook Dean that this dimension really exists, which I can do the moment I have a machine built.'

'Does your reinstatement rely on you doing this?'

'Not at all. I'm reinstated from this moment, but I'll be better pleased if I can show that old hidebound doyen what the other plane really looks like. Needless to say all police charges have been dropped. The trouble last night is now legally called a scientific accident. Well, that's my part of the happenings. Now, how about Vera? How's she faring?'

'I can give her fresh corneas for her eyes in three weeks.'

'You can!' Brooks' face lighted. 'Then she'll be able to see that machine again and ultimately we can go back over there.'

Douglas was silent, toying with the screws on his lens-grinding apparatus.

'My own restitution and name in lights carries a proviso,' he said slowly. 'Vera's eyes must be normal!'

'Normal! You — you mean blind to the fourth dimension?'

'Just that. You see the spot I'm in! On the one hand I want my vindication and to hand this eye discovery of mine to humanity. On the other hand I think we should go back over there. I just don't know which to do.'

Brooks clutched his arm tightly.

'Good grief, man, how can there even be a doubt in your mind as to what you

234

should do?' Brooks cried. 'What are a few petty honors from the Ophthalmic Council compared to what we can have in that other plane? A whole universe, if we play our cards right with Vera as the kingpin. You've got to give her the same eyes as before.'

For a long time Douglas stood meditating. Then he nodded.

'Okay, you're right. Now do me a favor, will you, and leave me to it? I've got to work on this job alone, give it all my concentration. You might slip over to the hospital and see Vera. She was asking for you.'

The physicist nodded and hurried out. Slowly Douglas drew off his coat and slipped into his white coverall. Going over to the safe he took out the precious formula he had devised for mitonex lenses and studied it. When its details began to return to his memory, he began to get to work.

To his satisfaction the job took him slightly under three weeks, and he was then given every facility to operate in the city hospital. Dr. Hurley had had a hand in this, however, and on the day of the operation he was present in the theater's observation balcony, staring down through plastic glass — in the company of his Ophthalmic Council colleagues — upon the table below, Douglas' masked and white-garbed figure and that of the attendant nurses beside it.

The most anxiously watching person of all was Mason Brooks. Immaculate, his dark hair gleaming as it lay back from his fine forehead, he stared down in concentrated attention from the balcony opposite that of the ophthalmic experts. A little distance away from him, also watching keenly, was Walbrook Dean, his rugged face in profile to Brooks' occasional glances.

The lights came up below in shadow-less glare. There was the glint of instruments in Douglas Ashfield's gloved hands. High in the roof television eyes, telescopic-lensed, were casting every detail of this amazing operation in optics to an interested world outside.

Douglas knew better than anybody else that he was throwing away world-fame even as he worked. Made to identically the same formula, the new cornea would not give single vision but, unless the immutable law of mathematics was a liar, precisely the same double vision as before.

Vera was not under a sleep-producing anesthetic this time. It was a purely local one with no sense of discomfort to her artificial eyes. But she was strapped down so tightly she could not budge her head a fraction of an inch.

Fixedly she stared into grayness, could feel Douglas' busy hands at work and the delicate probing of his instruments. Now and again she heard his strained voice giving sharp orders.

Suddenly one eye went totally black and a little chill stole to her heart. The other followed it and left her in a void that was infinitely dark and terrible.

'Nothing to worry about,' Douglas murmured in her ear. 'I have taken out the shattered corneas. You have no light-gathering capacity at the moment.'

He laid the broken corneas on one side with platinum-tipped forceps. Then working with infinite care he began the delicate job of sliding the new hemispheres into position under the girl's eyelids, after which they would remain in position by the natural suction of the eyeball's own curvature. The girl felt the edges sliding unbearably against her eyelids, despite the local anesthetic.

She gave a little cry as, with a transient stab of pain, the first cornea slipped into place and gentle, rubber-tipped fingers closed her eyelids tightly and laid wadding upon them. A brief pause followed. Then she went through the same experience with the other eye. This was closed, too, and cotton wadding placed on it and tied into position.

Straps began to unloose. She was raised gently by Douglas' arm at the back of her shoulders. Strong restorative began to burn in her throat.

Douglas waited a moment or two while the girl's nerves were steadying again and her pulse rate dropped to normal. Briskly he signaled to the watchers in the balconies. They turned and descended the rear stairs immediately, came filing into the theater.

'Excellent handling, Ashfield,' Hurley congratulated. 'Now for the results.'

'I think we are ready,' Douglas answered in quiet tones. For a moment his eyes strayed to the tense face of Mason Brooks as he stood rigid with anxiety.

The assembly waited. Douglas reached behind the girl's head and unfastened the tape. The wadding fell away.

'Open your eyes slowly,' Douglas ordered.

Vera obeyed, allowed her eyelids to flicker apart. When at last they were fully open there was a little gasp from the group of oculists. Her other eyes, before the breakage, had been marvelous imitations of the real thing, but these were even better. Either it lay in the curvature of the outer cornea, or in the lights of the theater, but there was a definite translucency. They were big, gray, and wondering. She stared steadily in front of her.

'Well?' Douglas asked tensely

'I can see — clearly, wonderfully!' she whispered. Her voice rose. 'Yes! Every detail of every thing, near and far, up or down. Far better than I ever saw in my life before! Oh, Doug dearest, you're the greatest eye-surgeon who ever lived.'

'Do you see double, or single?' her brother asked in a strained voice, coming to her side.

'Single, of course. Not a trace of anything else. I see as normally as you do.'

Brooks stared at her, his face going whiter than usual. Just for a second an outburst seemed to tremble on his lips. Then he forced the ghost of a smile.

'I'm so glad,' he said, almost inaudibly. 'For your sake. I'll — I'll see you later on.'

Hurley came forward and stared into the girl's eyes fixedly.

'Hmm, seem all right to me,' he commented. 'Are you prepared for our tests, Miss Brooks?'

'Surely,' the girl assented. 'But I'd prefer to sit in a chair instead of on this table.'

'Of course, of course.'

She was helped from the table into an armchair. Then under Hurley's directions apparatus was wheeled in from outside. The lights were switched off and for half an hour he and his fellow wizards of the optics studied and peered until she was dazzled by their lights and lenses. At last the illumination returned and she relaxed with a thankful sigh.

'You've done it, Doctor Ashfield,' Hurley pronounced, holding out his hand. 'The most brilliant optical advance of the century! The whole world shall hear of this. The city will make its gratitude known for you publicly at a banquet in your honor, at which Miss Brooks of course will also be present. You will be notified of the date through official sources. And thank you, Miss Brooks, for your cooperation. Come, gentlemen.'

They filed out, talking among themselves at the wonder they had witnessed. Then as the last man vanished from sight, the lone figure of Brooks came into view again. He came forward slowly, stopped at last within two feet of Douglas.

'What happened?' he asked bitterly.

Douglas did not answer. Instead he looked at the girl.

241

'You really mean that you can only see singly?' he demanded.

'On my word of honor,' she nodded. 'And I'm as surprised as you are. Anyway, I couldn't fool men like Hurley and his disciples with the apparatus they've got. My vision's dead normal.'

'Then what the devil went wrong?' Brooks exploded. 'Don't you realize what this means? Our last chance of seeing into the fourth dimension, of getting there again, has gone! I can never remember how to make a second transition machine from memory. Doug, what have you done, man?'

'I've followed out the cornea formula item for item,' he answered doggedly. 'It is the exact same material, the selfsame grinding, the selfsame field of focus and circle of vision. Everything is now just as it was before.'

'But it can't be!' Brooks shouted. 'It's different.'

'I know.' Douglas rubbed his chin slowly. 'Let's sum the thing up. The cornea was responsible for Vera seeing the fourth dimension. A slight aberration in its curvature altered the normal range of light-waves and she saw two planes. Now I have done the exact same formula over again, things are normal to her. There is only one possible explanation.'

'Well?' Brooks rasped.

'The grinding is not absolutely identical. It may only be a millionth of a fraction out on the orbit curvature but that, in the aggregate, means a lot. There are cases where spectacle lenses are made to an identical formula, yet the wearer swears he can see much clearer with one pair than with the other.

'The fault is not in the formula. It is in those infinitesimal details — a fraction out in the mechanism of the grinding equipment, a slightly less resistance in the surface of the lens material, even the action of temperature and humidity at the time of grinding. That is what must have happened here.

'The flaw which made a view of the fourth dimension possible has not happened again. It was, correctly, an unknown factor in my formula upon which I happened by chance, an unknown factor which

I may never find again unless once more it be by chance. Because, of course, I don't know what the factor is. It's something ungovernable, the outcome of a correlated series of conditions which happened that once, but which now . . . '

Douglas stopped, his lips compressed.

'We've lost the fourth dimension, I'm afraid,' he finished.

Brooks clenched his fists.

'You can explain this away by everyday circumstances, by flaws in the aggregate, if you like,' he snapped. 'But I believe only one thing is back of it — that confounded Presence! First my machine — now your inability to reproduce a fluke of optics, to say nothing of the way Vera's eyes were damaged in the transition back to this plane. The door has been slammed in our faces and locked good and hard!'

'That's possible,' Vera admitted. 'And I suppose it will stay locked until we learn the meaning of sense, peace, and science.'

The physicist breathed heavily as he paced up and down.

'The thought is too much to bear,' he insisted. 'All that wonderful science — a whole universe wide open before us, and now we've lost it! Just a glimpse of a mighty science, gone like a mirage. The marvels of generations have been blotted out with the finality of a falling star. It's abominable and unreasonable for it to be barred to us.'

'Just the same, it's gone,' Vera said quietly.

He looked at her for a long moment and gradually a cynical grin spread over his lean features.

'Out of all this I get reinstatement. That's damned funny!'

'And I'm famous.' Douglas gave a shrug. 'I would certainly have liked to have given people their four-dimensional heritage, but maybe it's a better thing to destroy the curse of blindness.'

Brooks sighed.

'Well, there it is! No good chasing rainbows, I guess. But I'll work myself as never before to find a way to duplicate that machine. I'm going back there — some day! No flaw in optics is going to stop me. And when I do — '

He broke off as he caught the eyes of

his sister and Douglas fixed upon him.

'I know, ambition,' he said dryly, nodding. 'Well then we'll forget it right now. At least we can celebrate four achievements — two reinstatements, new eyes, and a forthcoming marriage. How about a good dinner? Just to show there's no ill feeling, I'll stand the expense!'

THE END

CLIMATE INCORPORATED
THE FIVE MATCHBOXES
EXCEPT FOR ONE THING
BLACK MARIA, M.A.
ONE STEP TOO FAR
THE THIRTY-FIRST OF JUNE
THE FROZEN LIMIT
ONE REMAINED SEATED
THE MURDERED SCHOOLGIRL
SECRET OF THE RING

We do hope that you have enjoyed reading this large print book.

Did you know that all of our titles are available for purchase?

We publish a wide range of high quality large print books including:
Romances, Mysteries, Classics
General Fiction
Non Fiction and Westerns

Special interest titles available in large print are:
The Little Oxford Dictionary
Music Book, Song Book
Hymn Book, Service Book

Also available from us courtesy of Oxford University Press:
Young Readers' Dictionary
(large print edition)
Young Readers' Thesaurus
(large print edition)

For further information or a free brochure, please contact us at:
Ulverscroft Large Print Books Ltd.,
The Green, Bradgate Road, Anstey,
Leicester, LE7 7FU, England.
Tel: (00 44) **0116 236 4325**
Fax: (00 44) **0116 234 0205**

Other titles in the
Linford Mystery Library:

DRAGNET

Sydney J. Bounds

Johnny Fortune meets Ava Gray at the races, and learns that her sister Gail has become involved with a crooked bookmaker, Harvey Chandos. When Johnny helps her to bring Gail home, he's soon up against Nugent, a giant of a man, and Madame Popocopolis, the brain behind Chandos. Popocopolis's plan, to kidnap millionaire's son Roy Belknap for ransom money is thwarted when she finds herself at the centre of a police dragnet — wanted for murder . . .